"David deSilva's novel about a week in the life of Christians in Ephesus, living under the shadow of the Roman Empire, is a thrilling story as well as an educational journey through the ancient world. Set against the backdrop of the book of Revelation, this is not a novel that will leave you worried about being 'left behind,' but it will make a deep impression on how to be a faithful Christian against the backdrop of malevolent imperial power.... Could not put it down!"

Michael F. Bird, academic dean and lecturer in theology at Ridley College, Melbourne, Australia

"*A Week in the Life of Ephesus* brings alive the ancient Roman world of religious ritual, daily business, and family loyalties. The Christian's perennial challenge to follow after God and not money or fame takes shape under deSilva's skillful hand as first-century Ephesians live out their faith (or not) in the thoroughly pagan city. DeSilva weaves together characters, plot, and historical context, drawing the reader into the story. This is a must-read for those who want a deeper understanding of the ordinary reality of early Christians' lives."

Lynn H. Cohick, provost and dean, professor of New Testament, Denver Seminary

"Ephesus was one of the leading centers of Christianity in the ancient world, and David deSilva invites us to picture it through this imaginative recreation of first-century life. He is well known for his scholarship on Revelation, which addressed churches in Ephesus and other cities in the region. By weaving ancient source materials into his narrative and offering commentary along the way, he links the fictional story to the social world and archaeological remains of Ephesus. This is a resource for those who want a glimpse into the dilemmas faced by Jesus' followers in a complex urban environment."

Craig Koester, Nasby Professor of New Testament at Luther Seminary, St. Paul, Minnesota

"Prepare to be transported to the ancient city of Ephesus! David deSilva writes with a deft hand, proving that he is a gifted storyteller and cultural historian. Spend this week in Ephesus and you will read the New Testament with fresh eyes."

Joel B. Green, professor of New Testament interpretation at Fuller Theological Seminary

"Students and scholars have already enjoyed the meticulous historiography, sensitive literary analysis, imaginative flair, and theological depth of David DeSilva's previous writings, which range in genre from novel to New Testament introduction. In this volume, A Week in the Life of Ephesus, he conjoins these manifest strengths, taking the reader on an intriguing expedition to that ancient city in a crucial week of September in 89 CE. Through the eyes of ancient Christians in Ephesus, portrayed vividly in all their psychological and relational complexity, we come face-to-face with the perennial temptation to accommodate idolatry, with implications. DeSilva's compelling and suspe various strata of society is enhanced by hel offered in sidebars."

Edith M. Humphrey, William F. Orr Professor of I Seminary

"Using historical time travel brilliantly, deSilva incarnates the Christian community in Ephesus in the late first century AD. The challenges faced by believers—Christ versus Caesar, economic participation or marginalization, eating idol meat or abstaining—are effectively portrayed by characters known from texts and inscriptions. The reader feels the struggles of brothers and sisters trying to obey God as a fledgling minority while living in this political, commercial, and religious metropolis."

Mark Wilson, founder and director of the Asia Minor Research Center in Antalya, Turkey, author of *Biblical Turkey: A Guide to the Jewish and Christian Sites of Asia Minor*

"What a great book! What was it like to be a Christian in the city of Ephesus in AD 89? How did Christians respond to the challenges posed by life in this large Greco-Roman city with its gods and temples, markets and gymnasia? In this fictional narrative, David DeSilva helps us to enter into the world of believers in Jesus and to see their struggles and joys, their challenges and hopes. We see how various Christian groups responded differently to the pressures they faced, and in the process we come to understand the book of Revelation more deeply. You'll not want to put this book down!"

Paul Trebilco, professor of New Testament studies, University of Otago, Dunedin, New Zealand

"I often tell my students that one of our goals in New Testament courses is to develop our historical imaginations. Those accustomed to viewing faith and religion as a private sphere often struggle to imagine their way into the first-century world, where religion was deeply entwined with governmental structures and the corporate well-being of both city and empire. DeSilva's story narrates compellingly the very real pressure that early followers of Jesus would have experienced as many of their contemporaries viewed them as threats to the social order; if they refused to honor the gods, including the deified emperors, their reputations, finances, and even lives were at stake. Again and again in this story I asked myself, What would I have done?"

Holly Beers, associate professor of religious studies at Westmont College, author of *A Week in the Life of a Greco-Roman Woman*

"Drawing on his vast knowledge of the urban centers of Rome's empire and the all-powerful Roman religiopolitical machine, David deSilva vividly brings the world of Roman Ephesus to life. Readers are quickly and easily drawn into the material world of Ephesus, including its markets, harbor, neighborhoods, and grand temples, but they are also immersed in Ephesian religious fervor and piety. And it is in this world of religious fervor and piety the readers come not only to understand but also feel the immense pressure on Ephesian Christians to compromise their worship of the one creator God. DeSilva creatively casts this crisis of Christian faith as the setting for the book of Revelation. This superb piece of historical fiction will serve as a valuable asset for introducing students and laity to the urban world of first-century Christians and more specifically the world of the seven churches of John's Apocalypse."

Adam Winn, associate professor of Christian studies at the University of Mary Hardin-Baylor and author of *Killing a Messiah: A Novel*

A WEEK IN
THE LIFE OF
EPHESUS

DAVID A. DESILVA

ivp
Academic

An imprint of InterVarsity Press
Downers Grove, Illinois

InterVarsity Press
P.O. Box 1400, Downers Grove, IL 60515-1426
ivpress.com
email@ivpress.com

InterVarsity Press® is the book-publishing division of InterVarsity Christian Fellowship/USA®, a movement of students and faculty active on campus at hundreds of universities, colleges, and schools of nursing in the United States of America, and a member movement of the International Fellowship of Evangelical Students. For information about local and regional activities, visit intervarsity.org.

Figure 6.2 is used with permission courtesy of the Classical Numismatic Group, LLC. All other images are used with permission courtesy of the author.

Cover design: Cindy Kiple
Interior design: Beth McGill
Cover image: © MindStorm-inc / iStock / Getty Images Plus

ISBN 978-0-8308-2485-4 (print)
ISBN 978-0-8308-2537-0 (digital)

Printed in the United States of America ∞

InterVarsity Press is committed to ecological stewardship and to the conservation of natural resources in all our operations. This book was printed using sustainably sourced paper.

Library of Congress Cataloging-in-Publication Data
A catalog record for this book is available from the Library of Congress.

P 25 24 23 22 21 20 19 18 17 16 15 14 13 12 11 10 9 8 7 6 5 4 3 2 1
Y 41 40 39 38 37 36 35 34 33 32 31 30 29 28 27 26 25 24 23 22 21 20

To

DAVID W. BAKER, JOHN BYRON,
BRENDA B. COLIJN, WYNDY CORBIN REUSCHLING,
L. DANIEL HAWK, MICHAEL REUSCHLING,
DALE R. STOFFER, AND JOANN FORD WATSON—

*colleagues who have supported and sustained
me in so many ways during my tenure at
Ashland Theological Seminary*

CONTENTS

PREFACE

This book offers an imaginative re-creation of a few slices of the life of the city of Ephesus, particularly as experienced by a small number of families and connected individuals, in the last week of September in the year AD 89. Why I have chosen *that* week of all weeks will become clear as the story progresses. Like several of its predecessors in this series, this book seeks to open windows into the everyday, lived world of the kinds of people to whom books of the New Testament were written, or about whom the books of the New Testament might talk. It seeks to invite the modern reader into the concerns, interests, opportunities, and struggles that such people entertained or encountered.

This particular installment in the series is also a book about reading the Revelation of John. I have long suspected that many of my fellow Christians are quick to look to the Middle East, or China, or Russia, or the White House, or rumored technological advances, or wildfires in California, for the real-life counterparts to what they read in Revelation because they have had so little opportunity to immerse themselves in the world in which—and in the lives of the people *to whom*—Revelation was written. This story particularly seeks to highlight those facets of the life and landscape of Ephesus that loomed large in the lives of the late-first-century Christians there, whose perspectives on those facets of their lives Revelation affected profoundly (whether to confirm or confront).

I want to thank Dr. Dan G. Reid, formerly of InterVarsity Press, for so graciously receiving my proposal for this novella some years ago. As Dan transitioned into retirement, the responsibility for editing this book fell to his colleague Ethan McCarthy, whom I thank for his many valuable suggestions and his editorial acumen.

A work like the present one would hold far less value had it not been informed by spending significant time onsite. I am grateful to the trustees, administration, and faculty of Ashland Theological Seminary for a quarter's study leave in Spring 2011 and for a study-leave grant that supported my first travels in Turkey. Abdullah Gur, president of Meander Travel, very kindly made the arrangements for that visit, within which I had allotted three full days to explore Ephesus and Selçuk. As it was my first trip, he supplied me with a delightful guide, Mehmet Tanrıverdi, for my first days onsite at Ephesus, Izmir (Smyrna), and Pergamum and saw to my transportation between cities at his company's expense. James Ridgway, president of Educational Opportunities Tours, gave me the opportunity to return to Ephesus for a day's visit on three separate occasions in the context of larger Lands of the Bible and Journeys of Paul itineraries. I remain deeply grateful to both gentlemen and their highly competent staffs.

I have taught at Ashland Theological Seminary in Ohio since 1995. Drs. David Baker, Dale Stoffer, and Jody Watson had already been teaching there for several years when I arrived; Dr. Daniel Hawk joined the faculty with me; Dr. Brenda Colijn preceded me as a part-time instructor and came on full time after I arrived; and Drs. Michael Reuschling, Wyndy Corbin Reuschling, and John Byron followed not long afterward. In the event that I have not taken sufficient time along the way to tell these dear sisters and brothers how much I appreciate each of them and the many ways in which each has affected my life and sustained me in my work, I wish to do so now. So it is with deep gratitude for the collegiality we have discovered together over the decades that I dedicate this little book to them.

CHARACTERS IN THE DRAMA

Caius Flavius **Amyntas**, a Christian and wealthy landowner, grandson of a freedman

Tiberius Claudius **Aristion**, high priest and temple warden of the Temple of the Sebastoi

Burrhus, a Christian in Amyntas's house church

Chreste, the eleven-year-old daughter of Demetrius and Olympias

Flavia **Chrysanthe**, Amyntas's wife

T. Julius Damas **Claudianus**, a member of *koinon* (the provincial council) of Asia and president of the civic council of Ephesus

Demetrius, son of Apollonius, a Christian merchant and host to a house church

Diodotos, an outspoken Christian artisan and member of Amyntas's house church

Euplus, a Christian slave in Serapion's house

Fronto, a Christian in Amyntas's house church

Publius Aurelius **Hippicus**, son of Serapion and Isidora

Aurelia **Isidora**, Serapion's wife

Menes, a slave in the household of Amyntas

Titus Flavius **Montanus**, eventually to be associated with the titles "high priest of Asia's shared temple in Ephesos, *sebastophant*, and *agonothete* for life" in Ephesus

Nicolaus, son of Strato, of Pergamum, a Christian and junior priest of the Provincial Temple of Augustus and Roma in Pergamum

Olympias, Demetrius's wife

Parmenon, the steward in Serapion's household

Prochorus of Smyrna, a Christian and a disciple of John the Seer, assisting him in his exile on Patmos

Aulus Julius **Quadratus** of Pergamum, who would become proconsul of Asia in 108/109—now chief of staff of the proconsul of Asia, Marcus Gillo

Gaius Vibius **Salutaris**, a local benefactor

Caius Flavius **Secundus**, son of Amyntas and Chrysanthe

Publius Aurelius **Serapion**, a wealthy landowner and a priest of Artemis

Theon, the eight-year-old son of Demetrius and Olympias

Trophimus, a onetime associate of Paul, an elder among the Ephesian churches

Flavia **Tryphaina**, daughter of Amyntas and Chrysanthe

Titus Flavius **Zeuxis**, a successful sea captain and merchant, an imperial freedman, and a Jew

1

New Year's Day

1 Kaisaros, 9 Kalends October

The Divine Artemis Sends Birthday Wishes

Publius Aurelius Serapion, priest of Artemis, strode with pride past the crowd that had gathered outside the great Artemision for the sacred procession. A hundred or so had prescribed roles in the procession; a thousand more devotees had made the kilometer-and-a-half trek from the city's northern gate simply to participate.

He saw many faces in the crowd that were unfamiliar to him from his five decades of moving through the streets and fora of Ephesus, no doubt a good number of them tourists who had made their way here to see the temple that was lauded as one of the seven greatest architectural wonders of the world. Serapion recalled once seeing a visitor from Athens standing before the temple, weeping. He inquired of him what had affected him so.

"How can I now go back to Athens and take pride in our Parthenon? It would take four such houses of our goddess Athena to fill just this *one* of Artemis!"

Great indeed is Ephesian Artemis, Serapion mused with satisfaction.

Flanked by two acolytes bearing torches and clothed fully in white as he was, Serapion could feel his movements attract the attention of the crowd and savored the moment. It was no small honor to have been selected to lead the procession of Artemis on this day, and it was at no small cost to himself that he subsidized this honor, so he intended to enjoy it to the full. In the manner typical of Roman priests, he solemnly draped a fold of his freshly bleached cloak over his head before ascending the fourteen broad steps to the temple platform. Over a hundred columns stretched twenty meters toward the sky, forming a forest of marble before him as the great bronze doors of the sanctuary opened in a slow yawn at his approach. He and his attendants passed over the threshold and into a great hall lined with marble vaults on either side. In these were housed the wealth and treasures of Roman Asia's cities and nobility, the goddess herself standing as surety for their inviolable safety.

They passed into an open courtyard at the heart of the temple, at the far end of which stood the goddess's chamber. Her doors stood open this morning, and Serapion felt a surge of awe as he looked upon the great cult statue, standing fifteen meters tall. This was not Artemis as the Greeks imagined her, a young huntress with bow, quiver, and buskins, but an otherworldly Artemis, sporting the zodiac as her necklace, wearing dozens of winged griffins as her garment, adorned with several rows of eggs across her bosom as symbols of her life-giving bounty and fertility. On her head sat a crown representing the principal buildings of the city of Ephesus, for the city's fortunes indeed rested upon her strength and goodwill. Her arms were outstretched in a gesture of invitation, and Serapion felt himself indeed in the embrace of her favor this day.

In front of the great cult image stood a more portable manifestation of the goddess, a little more than two meters tall, attended now by a dozen young virgins, daughters of the Ephesian elite. They had already washed the goddess in pure water drawn from a nearby spring and anointed her face and hands with sacred oil. Now they were dressing her in fine silk vestments, as the professional priests who formed part of the temple staff looked on, instructing them in the ritual procedures. Twelve young men, also offspring from the best families, filed in to carry the goddess on her dais to the cart that awaited her in front of her temple. Serapion watched with pride as his own son, Hippicus, helped shoulder the divine load. One of the professional priests of the temple stood before both the

Figure 1.1. A cult image of Artemis found buried beneath the Prytaneion.

portable statue and the great cult image, raised his hands in a gesture of invocation, and prayed that the goddess would inhabit her smaller representation and travel with them to bless the city and to honor her divine colleague. He then nodded to Serapion to begin the procession.

Serapion led the way back toward the front of the sanctuary. As he emerged with his attendants through the great bronze doors, the image of Artemis hoisted aloft behind him, the musicians made their instruments sound, and the crowd burst into shouts of acclamation of the goddess. Serapion nodded to acknowledge his wife, Aurelia Isidora, who had been standing in attendance apart from the crowd with all of their household. Serapion had gone so far as to order the majority of the slaves from his estates in the countryside to travel into town and make his entourage the more impressive—at the cost of three days' productive labor on their part. As Serapion passed them, he registered the absence of one of his domestic slaves. A drop of adrenaline caused his pulse to quicken slightly as a wave of anger temporarily overwhelmed the more pleasant sensations of pride he had been indulging. He scanned the group again. *Euplus. He's not here.* Over the next twenty paces he worked to stifle his sense of outrage and compartmentalize his anger. *I will not allow that slave to cast a shadow over my enjoyment of this day's glory. And I will have satisfaction when next I see him.*

Serapion's honorary priestly colleagues—the *kourētai*, the small band of elite Ephesian males whose subvention of the cult purchased for them visibility, prestige, and influence—fell in line behind the cult image. They were followed by seven *aulētai*, who began to blow the melody of a familiar hymn to Artemis through their reed-pipes over the harmonies of seven harpists playing on their *kitharas*, who fell in step behind them, followed by a choir of fourteen voices reciting hymns that told of Artemis's virtues and mighty deeds on behalf of the world. Young men carrying torches spaced themselves out along the procession between women carrying baskets full of cereal offerings and incense, teenage girls dressed in hunting attire leading hounds on leashes, and temple servants leading a bull with garlands made from woven vines and flowers adorning it. Serapion's household took their place next, at the head of the throng of worshipers who would follow.

It took a full half-hour for the procession to cross the marshy plain on the raised dirt path leading from the temple to the city, swatting insects as they walked. *No greater benefaction could be given to the city than a paved road—perhaps even a* covered,

MUSICAL INSTRUMENTS IN THE ROMAN PERIOD

The principal wind instrument was the *aulos* (Latin *tibia*). The aulos consisted of two separate pipes, each with a double reed in one end as the source of the resonance; a hole on the underside, where the thumb rested; and five holes on the upper side (only four of which could ever be covered by the fingers). Each pipe thus had the capacity to sound six different notes. It is not entirely clear how the *aulētēs* would play his or her aulos. The prevailing theory is that both pipes were played in unison. Two pipes were played because the imperfect tuning of the instruments created a bolder sound. It is also possible that different notes were played on each pipe, or that the aulētēs could alternate a drone effect on either pipe while playing melody on the other.[a] *Auloi* were crafted in different sizes, similar to the family of recorders in the modern period (sopranino, soprano, alto, tenor, bass, and contrabass).

The name given to the pan flute suggests an origin in ancient Greece, though this instrument was known as the *syrinx*. In the classical world, the pipes were all of the same length. The pipes were made

Figure 1.2. A young woman playing the aulos.

to sound at different pitches by being filled to a different level with bees-wax. There was also a kind of transverse flute crafted by drilling mouth and fingering holes into a hollow reed. Because both hands could cover holes on a single pipe, the flute had a range of ten notes.

The two principal stringed instruments were the kithara and the lyre. The kithara—the "harp" commonly encountered in Revelation (Rev 5:8; 14:2; 15:2) and an emblem of the god Apollo—was made of a single piece of wood, typically with seven strings stretched over the hollowed-out soundboard. The lyre resembled the kithara, save that it was frequently constructed of a wooden frame inserted into a tortoise shell, which functioned as the resonator box. Both appear to have been played by a combination of plucking particular strings with the

left hand and strumming with a plectrum held in the right hand (with the possibility of dampening certain strings with the left hand).

The *salpinx*, or trumpet (see 1 Cor 14:8; 15:52; Rev 8:2, 6), was essentially a thin metal tube about a meter long with a ball-like bell in the Greek period and the more familiar flared bell in the Roman

Figure 1.3. Apollo holding a kithara.

period. It had no keys, so the player could only sound notes in the harmonic scale (octaves, fifths, and eventually high thirds) by manipulating the tension on his or her lips and thus the speed with which they vibrated at the head of the column of air in the tube. The Romans developed a circular version of this, the *cornu*, which had the same limitations.

Greeks and Romans also had a number of percussion instruments at their disposal. Most basic was the *tympanon*, a hand drum made by stretching animal skin over a round frame. Singers and dancers might also employ *krotala*, essentially a precursor of the castanet, or *cymbala*, a smaller and thicker version of the cymbals familiar to us that produced a higher pitch (see 1 Cor 13:1). A kind of rattle called a *sistrum* was emblematic of the cult of the Egyptian goddess Isis; similar instruments might have been used in broader contexts. And, of course, there was the gong (1 Cor 13:1).

[a]See the more complete discussion in John G. Landels, *Music in Ancient Greece and Rome* (London: Routledge, 1999), 41-46. Landels provides a thorough treatment of all the instruments named here as well as a musical analysis of surviving pieces of ancient notation, with several reconstructions of ancient hymns and songs.

paved road—from the Artemision to the city's two principal gates, Serapion thought. It had been discussed many times in the Bouleuterion, but other civic priorities continued to claim all the disposable funds of leading citizens of any magnitude. *At least the rains haven't started yet.*

They came at last to the southeastern gate of the city, the one whose road led east to Magnesia and then to Tralles and Laodicea. The procession passed through the city's fortification wall, up a street lined with small shops, and began pouring at last into the civic forum. The broad, open pavement was about the size of the Artemision, surrounded by columned porticoes and civic offices and public buildings. On any other day, this was the administrative and judicial nerve center of the city. Today, however, it was the sacred courtyard of the Temple of Dea

Roma and Divus Augustus, the goddess Roma and the deified
Augustus.[1] The space had been thronged already with several
thousand worshipers, though city officials had maintained a
wide, open path through the forum and a large space before the
Augusteion specifically for this procession.

Figure 1.4. The excavated foundations of the Temple of Divus Augustus and Dea Roma.

[1]The precise identification of the temples of Divus Julius and Divus Augustus in the
Ephesian civic forum is a matter of debate. Peter Scherrer argues that the freestanding
temple in the center of the forum was the Temple to Divus Julius and Dea Roma decreed to be built there by Augustus in 29 BC, when Ephesus was made the capital of
the province, while a double temple between the Prytaneion and Bouleuterion was
dedicated to Augustus and Artemis. See Scherrer, *Ephesus: The New Guide* (Istanbul:
Ege Yayınları, 2000), 4-5; Scherrer, "The City of Ephesos from the Roman Period to
Late Antiquity," in *Ephesos: Metropolis of Asia*, ed. Helmut Koester, Harvard Theological Studies 41 (Valley Forge, PA: Trinity Press International, 1995), 1-25. Steven
Friesen and S. R. F. Price, however, argue for the identification adopted here (with the
smaller temple beside the Prytaneion being dedicated to Artemis and Julius Caesar).
See Friesen, *Twice Neokoros: Ephesus, Asia, and the Cult of the Flavian Imperial Fam-
ily* (Leiden: Brill, 1993), 11n21; Friesen, *Imperial Cults and the Apocalypse of John:
Reading Revelation in the Ruins* (Oxford: Oxford University Press, 2001), 101; Price,
Rituals and Power: The Roman Imperial Cult in Asia Minor (Cambridge: Cambridge
University Press, 1984, 254).

As he led the goddess into the forum, Serapion's eyes first fell on the bath complex in its northeast corner—which he would be sure to visit after the morning's festivities were concluded. To its west he scanned the Basilica Stoa, a great three-aisled hall built for the city by Sextus Pollio nearly a century ago. Typically a venue where magistrates and, on occasion, where the governor himself heard legal cases, today it was filled with Ephesians who had come to witness the main events in the forum. An inscription carved above its outer columns in letters the size of a forearm across the entire architrave read: "To Artemis of the Ephesians; Emperor Caesar Augustus, son of a god; Tiberius Caesar, son of Augustus; and to the Ephesian people."[2] It was the perfect backdrop for today's annual event, Serapion mused, for Artemis of the Ephesians had come out with her retinue this morning specifically to pay her respects to the deceased-yet-deified Emperor Caesar Augustus on his birthday.

The *aulētai* and kitharists reached a cadence and fell silent as Serapion, his attendants, and the goddess moved forward into the space before the divine Augustus's temple. A row of Ephesian noblemen, the folds of their cloaks also draped over their heads, stood before the Augusteion in a V-shaped formation surrounding a small, flaming altar. Each held a shallow bowl in his right hand. One of them, an elderly gentleman whose girth seemed merely a physical manifestation of his great ego, stepped forward from the center of the formation, and Serapion addressed the man in his most sonorous and solemn intonations.

"Julius Damas Claudianus, worthy priest of our great god Augustus: our great goddess Artemis, protectress of Ephesus, patroness of the Ephesian people, and friend to all who are friends of Rome, brings greetings to her divine colleague, the god Augustus Caesar, on this, the anniversary of his holy birth."

---

[2]Friesen, *Imperial Cults*, 95.

Serapion extended his arms, gesturing to gifts that were not yet visible. At his cue, the maidens bearing grain and incense came forward. The temple priest followed, leading the garlanded bull to the iron ring beside the altar, to which he securely tethered its neck.

"Publius Aurelius Serapion, holy and honorable *kourētēs* of the great goddess Artemis: our great god Augustus, bringer of peace to the whole world, welcomes his divine colleague and

---

ROMAN ASIA'S CALENDAR

Like most of Alexander's empire, the city of Ephesus grew accustomed to using the Macedonian calendar. With the advent of Roman rule, the Macedonian calendar (like local calendars elsewhere in the Roman Empire) coexisted with the Roman calendar. The latter was itself brilliantly reformed by Julius Caesar between 47 and 45 BCE, bringing the Roman year and the solar year into closer synchronism than ever before and eliminating the need for adding an extra (short) month every other year.

In or around 9 BC, the Provincial Assembly of Asia proposed a contest—a victor's wreath for the person who could devise the most appropriate honors for the emperor Augustus. The winner was Paullus Fabius Maximus, the Roman proconsul of Asia at the time. He recommended that Asia adopt a new calendar—reordering its very sense of time—around Augustus. He reasoned that, since Augustus's accession to rule marked the beginning of a new era of peace and prosperity for the whole world, Augustus's birthday would henceforth be appropriately considered Asia's New Year's Day, a perpetual reminder of the new beginning he gave to all. Local officials would begin their terms of office henceforth on that day as well. At the same time, the name of the (new) first month of the Macedonian calendar year was to be changed from

extends his gratitude to her for renewing their friendship by her visit this day and by these gifts, worthy of a god, worthily given by a god."

The maidens each dropped to one knee, bowed their heads, and held their baskets aloft. The priests of Augustus now came forward in two lines, some scooping up a portion of grain, others a portion of incense, from the baskets and circled inward to approach the flaming altar. Each in turn poured out the contents

---

Dios, named in honor of Zeus, to Kaisaros, with the first day of Kaisaros falling on September 23, Augustus's birthday.

The assembly's decree in support of the proposal is nothing short of messianic, praising the recommendation because

> the Providence that sets all the things pertinent to our lives in order, showing diligent care and extravagance, bestowed the most perfect adornment on life by offering us Augustus, whom she filled with excellence to benefit humanity, even as she sent to us and to those after us [a Savior] who would make war to cease and order [all things]. . . . The day of the god's birth constituted for the world the beginning of the good news that would come about through him.[a]

The decree itself was carved in white marble and set up in the provincial temple of Rome and Augustus in Pergamum as well as imperial shrines in district capitals and beyond. The most substantial physical remains of the inscription were found at Priene, which has given its name to the inscription.

---

[a]Translation mine. See further Friesen, *Imperial Cults,* 32-35; F. W. Danker, *Benefactor: Epigraphic Study of a Graeco Roman and New Testament Semantic Field* (St. Louis: Clayton, 1982), 215-22.

of his bowl over the fire, the grain sending up flaming cinders and the incense clouds of smoke, the fragrance of which began to fill the courtyard.

Another man in priestly attire, who looked to be about Serapion's age, stepped forward. He was unknown to Serapion, but he was clearly an imperial priest. His black-and-gray locks flowed out from under a metal headband bearing miniature busts of the goddess Roma and the divine Augustus, visible beneath the fold of his cloak that he had draped over his head. He stood tall and confidently before the bull and extended his right hand, fingers outstretched, before its eyes.

"Do you consent to be given to the god Augustus?" the priest inquired of the animal. As he pivoted his hand up and down at his wrist, the bull followed it, thus appearing to nod in approval.

The priest deftly sliced the bull's jugular with the curved blade he held in his left hand, and an attendant stepped forward with a basin to catch a portion of the blood as the priest from the Artemision dispatched the animal quickly with a hammer's blow to the skull. The animal collapsed instantly to the ground. The priest of Augustus from Pergamum received the basin and turned to pour its contents slowly over the flame, so that the fire evaporated the liquid before the latter could quench the fire, symbolically transferring the bull to the birthday god. At this, a choir of young Ephesian men began to chant a hymn in the god's honor.

> *A new year begins today*
> *even as, one hundred and fifty-three years past,*
> *a new age had begun on this day*
> *with Augustus's birth—then mere Octavianus,*
> *whom no one yet suspected was destined by the gods,*
> *in their unfailing goodwill toward humanity,*
> *to usher in an everlasting peace on earth*

through the everlasting dominion of Rome,
the great anchor for the circle of the lands,
the stabilizing power that brought prosperity
back for all peoples. . . .

When the hymn had ended, the goddess took her leave of her divine colleague through her mouthpiece, Serapion, who then led the procession on to complete the remainder of its circuit through the city. He and his torchbearers conducted Artemis and her lengthy entourage past the Augusteion toward the northwest corner of the civic forum. There they began their descent down the street called the Embolos, the "wedge," since it cut diagonally across the normal grid pattern of the streets on its way to the lower city—the commercial and entertainment districts. Serapion passed first a series of smallish monuments, with a great square opening up on the left—the principal approach to the new Temple of Domitian, the living emperor and god, the inaugural ceremonies for which were just a month away and occupying the attention of the greater part of the city's elite. A few more strides and he was surrounded by shops on both sides of the street, with tightly packed residential buildings crawling up the hillsides above them. Some residents appeared at the thresholds of their shops, burning incense on small portable altars to honor the goddess as she passed by. Interspersed among them along the sides of the road were statues of long-deceased residents, honorific inscriptions below them perpetually proclaiming their generosity or service toward their city.

As the procession neared the lower end of the Embolos, Serapion looked up and to the left, where his own sprawling townhouse was located. On a rooftop terrace just below his own, he caught sight of his neighbor, Caius Flavius Amyntas, watching the procession as it approached. He felt a sudden rush of indignation, remembering all at once his neighbor's conspicuous withdrawal from all things properly pious and the strange incantations that rose from his dwelling on the night of the first day of every week. He could not continue to allow impiety to go unchallenged in his city, so he halted the procession.

"What's this, Amyntas?" Serapion called out conspicuously, feigning surprise. "Not joining in the sacred rites of our city— today of all days?"

"Your pardon, most esteemed Serapion. I had wanted to come but have been unwell since last night."

Unwell indeed . . . since you caught that sick superstition.

"My prayers have been rising alongside your own today," Amyntas added. "Of that you can be assured."

A number of the onlookers, satisfied with this expression of piety, waved and wished him good health, turning their attention back to Serapion in expectation of the latter's resumption of his course. Serapion smirked knowingly at Amyntas and allowed the procession to advance. As he turned the corner onto the street that would take him past the great theater, Serapion glanced back over his shoulder once more at Amyntas.

Artemis, he prayed silently, *cleanse your city—and especially its nobility—of the foul infections of impiety, and hold not their presence among us against us.*

A Symposium in the Prytaneion

His duties to Artemis fulfilled, Serapion spent the early hours of the afternoon in the baths, then retired to his townhouse at the base of the Embolos to prepare himself for the evening's festivities. His prominent role in the day's rites assured him an invitation to dinner with the city fathers and visiting dignitaries. With the sun setting behind him, Serapion made his way back up the Embolos toward the civic forum.

He walked past several smaller parties as groups of friends and associates, well supplied with meat from the many animals sacrificed earlier in the day along with bread and ample wine provided at public expense, gathered around fires in the front rooms of shops or in smaller courtyards. As he neared the top of the Embolos, he could hear the sounds of larger gatherings of locals in the civic forum and smell the pleasant odor of meat roasting on many fires.

Figure 1.5. The Embolos, in the direction of the civic forum.

He headed toward the first large public building on his left—
the Prytaneion, the "hearth" of the city on the corner of the
civic forum. As he crossed its forecourt, he looked with satisfaction upon its front columns, into which had been carefully
inscribed hundreds of names. He paused at the threshold to
touch his own name, not far above the blank column drums
that would be engraved with the names of future colleagues
and successors in this priesthood. He continued past the sacred
hearth burning in the vestibule, attended perpetually by two of
the city-owned slaves in twelve-hour shifts, through a sacred
cult hall, and into the dining facilities to the rear of the complex.
He stood before three large couches arranged as three sides of
a square around a low table.

"Welcome, Publius Aurelius Serapion," announced the elderly
priest of Augustus who had presided over the morning's liturgy.

"My thanks, noble Julius Damas Claudianus," he replied.

"Please join us here on my couch," Claudianus said, slightly
raising himself from the cushions with his left arm and beck-
oning with his right. "I am acting as host tonight in the absence
of our illustrious proconsul, Marcus Fulvius Gillo, though he
has spared us his chief of staff, Aulus Julius Quadratus of Pergamum, here to my right. As one of the *kourētai* of Artemis—
and perhaps the only person present who is officially attached
to the Prytaneion—it is fitting that you also occupy a place at
the host's couch."

Serapion smiled at Claudianus's gentle attempt to soften the
blow of not being given the vacant seat at the middle couch, the
place for the most honored guests, and took the place nearest
him on the couch to his left. He had barely situated himself when
another man—the imperial priest from Pergamum who had
overseen the sacrifice of Artemis's bull—entered the hall.

"I hope I've not kept you waiting."

Figure 1.6. A column drum from the Prytaneion showing the inscribed names of priests and other office holders.

Figure 1.7. The forecourt of, and entrance into, the Prytaneion.

THE TITLE *NEŌKOROS*

During the classical and Hellenistic periods, the *neōkoros* was a functionary in Greek temples whose duties might best be compared to that of custodian or sexton in modern churches. The title itself meant "temple sweeper." Its usage and meaning changed in the late Hellenistic and early Roman periods and came to refer to a temple's primary benefactor for some term, generally a citizen who undertook a major role in underwriting the cost of the upkeep or other major expenses of a temple and its cultic activities, often enjoying therefore the honor and prestige of assisting in the rites performed. It is therefore often translated as "temple warden" or "temple keeper."

Ephesus began to use the title to describe its relationship to the great Artemision, which sat less than a mile from its city walls and with which it enjoyed a particularly close association (see Acts 19:35). The goddess worshiped there was, after all, Diana/Artemis of the Ephesians, as attested not only by the record of Acts 19:28, 34 but by many provincial and civic coin mintings that celebrated *Diana Ephesia* on their reverses. It came to be applied informally at some point

Figure 1.8. An inscription from the reign of Trajan in which Ephesus describes itself as a *neōkoros* city.

in the first century specifically to cities that were awarded the right to host the province-wide cult of a particular emperor. By the time Ephesus constructed its temple for the provincial cult of the Flavian household, this meaning had become more or less the technical sense of the term.

"Not at all," Claudianus assured him. "Gentlemen, this is Nicolaus, son of Strato, of Pergamum, one of the assistant priests of the Temple of the Goddess Roma and the Divine Augustus there, who was so kind as to grace our ceremonies today on the birthday of the god."

The other guests voiced their greetings as Nicolaus removed his outer cloak and handed it to an attendant.

"Since this is Augustus's birthday, and since you come as a representative of the leading temple dedicated to his worship in our province, it is only fitting that you be given the highest place tonight."

"I am honored indeed, noble Claudianus," said Nicolaus as he took the position on the middle couch closest to the host.

"We have assigned places of honor alongside you to our esteemed guests from Smyrna—Claudius Aristophanes Aurelianus and Julius Menekleus Diophantes," Claudianus said, indicating the other two men on the middle couch. "Both are priests associated with the Provincial Temple of Tiberius, Livia, and the Senate in Smyrna; Aurelianus is a colleague of mine on the provincial council as well. But these three men here," Claudianus said as he turned toward the couch opposite his own and gestured toward its occupants to give added weight to his words, "are the best men, the *first* men, in Ephesus."

The oldest of the three made a pantomime of objecting.

"No, Aristion, it's true, and there's no point denying it," Claudianus went on. "This gentleman is Tiberius Claudius Ariston, who has been named high priest and warden of our Temple of Domitian *and* gymnasiarch-elect of the Harbor Gymnasium, still unfortunately under construction, in recognition of his prominent and significant support underwriting both projects."[3]

---

[3]Tiberius Claudius Ariston is known from inscriptions in Ephesus to have been an active leader in the cult of Domitian at its inauguration and for decades after. He went on to

The others prevented Claudianus from continuing by cheering Aristion both for his munificence and for the signal honors it won for him.

"Well deserved, well deserved," Claudianus said, affirming the interruption. "And next to him is Titus Flavius Montanus, whose devotion and generosity toward the Temple of Domitian and its associated rites has also distinguished him above his peers. In recognition of this, he has been named *sebastophant* of the imperial mysteries of the divine Domitian and *agonothetēs* for life of the imperial games that shall be held in honor of the divine Domitian here every two years.[4] And next to him is Gaius Vibius Salutaris, another gentleman whose piety and benefactions show him to be a true friend of Artemis and a friend of Caesar."[5]

Nicolaus exchanged greetings with the three Ephesian dignitaries.

"Of course you know Quadratus, your fellow Pergamene. There beside him is Publius Aurelius Serapion, another citizen of Ephesus."

"Yes, the priest of Artemis who officiated with such piety and decorum this morning," Nicolaus acknowledged. Serapion nodded appreciatively.

Two slaves who had been waiting for Claudianus's signal came forward, one bearing a small brazier and the other a cup of wine and shallow bowl with a small amount of crushed incense. The

---

hold most of the major public offices in Ephesus through at least AD 112. See Friesen, *Twice Neokoros*, 162-63; J. Nelson Kraybill, *Imperial Cult and Commerce in John's Apocalypse* (Sheffield: Sheffield Academic, 1996), 70, 114. Claudianus is also named in an inscription as a leader in the provincial assembly and imperial cult in the 90s (Friesen, *Twice Neokoros*, 162), though nothing more of his biography is known.

[4]Titus Flavius Montanus is known from an inscription to have held these offices as well as the office of high priest of the Flavian temple at some point between AD 90 and 112 (Friesen, *Imperial Cults*, 114).

[5]An inscription in Ephesus names a Gaius Vibius Salutaris as *philartemis kai philokaisar*, "a friend of Artemis and friend of Caesar," as evidenced by some benefaction of his.

first placed the brazier in front of Claudianus on the table, while the second handed him the bowl of incense. Raising himself again with his left arm, he emptied the bowl over the fire. He gave the bowl back to the slave and took the cup into his right hand.

"We give thanks to the goddess Hestia, protector of hearth and home, in whose sacred precincts we meet."

Claudianus poured a small amount of wine over the fire.

"We give thanks to the goddess Artemis, protector of Ephesus and guarantor of its future."

He poured the wine a second time.

"Above all this day, we give thanks to the god Augustus, through whom Providence has established the new world order, this golden age of peace and prosperity. May it endure forever, world without end."

Claudianus emptied the goblet over the brazier, which the slave then dutifully removed as a line of female slaves entered with goblets of wine and water for each guest and several plates of their first courses—bread made from the finest ground wheat, still steaming from the oven; a variety of olives, cheeses, and nuts; and slices of tomato, cucumber, and eggplant marinated in wine and herbs.

"Marcus Fulvius Gillo, our noble proconsul, sends his personal greetings to each one of you and his regrets that he could not entertain you personally on your visit," Quadratus announced on his behalf. "As most of you are aware, he has been in Pergamum for the celebration of the divine Augustus's birthday at the provincial temple there."

"And in our city," Nicolaus added, "the celebration of the anniversary of the divine Augustus's birth is part of a *three*-day event that began two days ago on the birthday of his wife, the divine Livia Augusta. Your *one*-day festival is more on the scale of our monthly celebration on the first day of every month."

Serapion raised an eyebrow as he reached for some bread and goat cheese, wondering which of his fellow citizens would take the bait.

"It's only proper, of course, for the provincial center of Augustus's cult to celebrate in the most lavish manner," Aristion replied, a little defensively. "I expect that our celebrations in honor of the birthday of our lord and god Domitian next month, and ever after, will outpace those of the rest of Asia Minor taken as a whole."

"Laodicea has almost completed its local temple honoring Domitian," Aurelianus of Smyrna reported. "It promises to be quite magnificent."

"Magnificent?" Aristion hissed, inflating slightly like a provoked toad. "Before you leave here, you will see a temple worthy of being called 'magnificent,' a temple worthy of the divine Domitian and worthy of a *neokorate* city."

"Yes," Claudianus interjected in an attempt to direct the conversation away from the perpetual civic rivalry, "we've arranged for you all to tour the sacred precincts of the new temple—Asia's Shared Temple of the Augusti in Ephesus, as the provincial council has named it.[6] Aristion, where do we stand in our preparations?"

Aristion allowed himself to deflate into a more relaxed demeanor.

"The temple's chief offices and most supporting ones have been filled. A few remain vacant, including a position in the council of *neopoioi* opened up by the untimely death of Lucius Claudius Philometor."

"In terms of financing the cult, we could do just fine without the full complement," Montanus added, "but we want our support base to be as strong as possible as we inaugurate the new temple."

"We plan to take up the matter tomorrow when the city council meets," Aristion declared as three slaves returned to

---

[6]This is the title given to the complex in dedicatory inscriptions placed on the premises by other cities in the Roman province of Asia (Friesen, *Imperial Cults*, 45-46).

clear the table of the platters of appetizers, now well picked over. "Final preparations for the rites themselves and for the inaugural games are also well in hand, even though the new bath facilities by the harbor will not be ready in time to accommodate the athletes competing in the first Domitianic Games. The training grounds, at least, will be serviceable."

"I'm certain the baths in the gymnasium beyond the theater will suffice," Serapion said reassuringly.

"Do let us know," Claudianus added, "if either Aurelianus of Smyrna here or I myself can offer help in any way. As members of the provincial council entrusted with the oversight of all these cult centers, we want nothing to be lacking. The more thoughtfulness and resources we put into these shrines and their rites, the greater the honor and imperial favor enjoyed by the whole province."

"And this new Temple of Domitian has brought significant recognition to the great city of Ephesus at long last," Aurelianus added. "I've noticed the newer inscriptions of civic decrees around the city written in the name of 'the council and people of the temple-warden city of the Ephesians,' putting your enjoyment of the honor front and center in your self-identification."

"The honor's been too long deferred," complained Salutaris. "Ephesus, the home of the great Artemision, the capital city of the Roman province! We should have been awarded an imperial neokorate decades ago."

"It's no secret, Aurelianus, that we are proud indeed," Montanus admitted "to have gained at last the same distinction that you in Smyrna and your neighbors in Pergamum enjoy."

"There are still *distinctions* to be made among distinctions," Quadratus interjected.

Aristion and Montanus looked across at the chief of staff quizzically.

"Ah," Nicolaus said with a slightly embarrassed smile. "My fellow citizen refers to a fresh inscription in our own city recording a decree by 'the council and people of the first-to-be-awarded-a-temple-wardenship city of the Pergamenes.'"

The company enjoyed a good laugh at the clever one-up-manship—all save for Aristion, who was clearly not amused.

"Let's suspend our rivalries for one evening," Claudianus said diplomatically, "and savor our common boast that our *three* cities enjoy the distinction of hosting the only three provincial temples of the imperial cult in Roman Asia to date. Local temples to the deified emperors may abound throughout the province, but the emperors themselves made the selection of our three fair cities to receive the title of *neōkoros*, and to be the guardians and perpetuators of their cult."

The Ephesians, Smyrnaeans, and Pergamenes raised cups of wine to one another and drank to their success in rising to the top places in the province, however disputed the rankings within that top circle might remain.

Claudianus signaled once again to the steward, who disappeared momentarily from view.

"The chief priest of the provincial temple of Rome and Augustus in Pergamum will be here personally to celebrate the rites in the Ephesian Augusteion on the first day of next month," Nicolaus announced, "the day before the inaugural rites of your splendid temple on the birthday of our lord and god Domitian."

"I have learned of this," Aristion said, "and wish to extend to him the honor and courtesy of taking part with me in the inaugural ceremonies in Domitian's temple."

The Prytaneion's slaves now emerged with trays bearing the main courses.

"We have reserved the choicest parts of this day's sacrifices for your pleasure tonight, gentlemen," Claudianus announced, nodding to the steward for the details.

Gesturing toward each dish in turn, the steward announced: "Roasted tenderloins of beef accompanied by a wine and juniper glaze; thinly sliced beef heart, slow-cooked in a well-herbed broth; beef liver, minced and flash-fired with garlic, onion, and olives; and the sweetbreads, poached and pan-seared in oil seasoned with ginger and wine. I pray that our efforts delight you."

"We give thanks again to the divine Augustus," Claudianus said dutifully, "for allowing us to share his table this day."

As the slaves served portions of each dish to the guests and filled the cups again with wine, Serapion screwed up the nerve to raise a delicate issue.

"I am delighted that my city now has the honor of a provincial temple, and I, for one, would not begrudge Pergamum its claim to hold preeminence for being the first among us to propose such honors for an emperor a century ago."

He paused a moment to chew thoughtfully.

"I do, however, begrudge the presence of people in our midst for whom the gods mean nothing, who regard the honors we show our emperors as an empty show and look with contempt upon our celebrations today."

Aurelianus was the first to guess at Serapion's meaning.

"You're referring to the Jews in our cities? Those narrow-minded, antisocial atheists who think our gods to be so many sticks and stones?"

A number of Aurelianus's fellow diners snorted their assent to his inference—and his characterization of the monotheists in their midst.

"Jews are *born* into their folly," Serapion replied. "Our noble emperors have granted them toleration, even affirming their rights after their disgraceful revolt against the Roman peace. I'm thinking rather of once-honest, gods-fearing Greeks and Romans turning their backs on religion."

"The Christ cult," ventured Nicolaus.

"Precisely."

"But they're just another Jewish faction, aren't they?" Claudianus objected.

"That's not what the Jewish community in Smyrna would say," interjected Aurelianus. "They've made it quite clear that we are not to associate the Christ-followers in Smyrna with them."

"Which leaves me wondering why we continue to tolerate them in our midst," said Serapion. "Our cities vie with one another to house a particular temple to a particular emperor, and then turn a blind eye to pockets of our populations who spit on our temples and our piety. If the emperor were to learn of this, he would be right to blame us for not enforcing unity and proper religion among our cities' people."

Several around the triclinium nodded and grunted their assent to Serapion's implicit challenge.

Nicolaus could not permit the consensus to go unchallenged. "We were speaking a few moments ago about the importance of observing distinctions. I would urge you to take care not to paint every member of a group in the same colors."

"What do you mean, Nicolaus?" asked Claudianus.

"Gentlemen, would it surprise you to learn that I myself am a devotee of the *Christos*?"

Their silence said that it had.

At last Serapion ventured, suspecting that the Pergamene was playing a joke on them, "How can you be a Christian *and* a priest of Augustus?"

"Not all who bear the name 'Christian' deny the gods and our emperors their due. Indeed, the *Christos* himself had taught his disciples, while he was a mortal on earth, to give to God what belonged to God and to give to Caesar what was rightly Caesar's."

Claudianus did not suppress a surprised grunt at this new information. The other dignitaries sat in silent attention to hear more of this explanation.

"Some Christians, I grant you, are tainted by the same atheism that characterizes the Jewish people from among whom the *Christos* himself came, but this is far from universal. Other Christians—like myself—can be just as supportive of the authorities on whom our common prosperity depends as anyone else, and just as dutiful toward the gods." Nicolaus pressed his case further. "There are a good number of Christ-followers in Pergamum who are of the same mind—and in Thyatira as well, I know for a fact. A woman of some means there has helped curb the exclusivist tendencies of the group and nurtured a more wholesome respect for the city's pantheon."

"What, then," Serapion asked, "is the attraction of this foreign superstition to a man like yourself?"

"We can all acknowledge our dependence upon the gods and the divine emperors for the preservation of the state and our common well-being. But what about our individual fates in this world and, even more pressing, on the other side of death? The *Christos* died and returned to life to bring assurance that death is not the end and that fear of death need not tyrannize us throughout our lives. For this gift I honor him, even as I honor our emperors for their great benefactions toward humankind."

"Your own position in the cult of Augustus leaves me no room to contradict you," Serapion conceded, "but not all known to be Christians in Ephesus are so pious as yourself."

"I would simply ask you, most of whom are colleagues alongside me in the cult of the emperors, not to judge any group by its ugliest members. If all were to be judged thus, what group, what race, what city, would escape a bad reputation?"

"A fair point, Nicolaus," Claudianus acknowledged. "The gods of Rome are not jealous of other gods—as long as those gods are not jealous of the gods of Rome."

The other guests nodded their approval of Nicolaus's explanation. Claudianus signaled the steward once again, and the slaves of the Prytaneion cleared away the remains of the main course, brought bowls of water for the guests to wash their fingertips, and began to set out varieties of local fruits, sliced and served with nuts and date honey. Cups were refilled with wine, and conversation continued long into the night about local and provincial politics.

Serapion could not keep himself from musing throughout the evening, however, about what deeper enmity against the public good lurked in the heart of his neighbor Amyntas when other Christians, such as this Nicolaus, had no difficulty giving the gods their due.

2

Roman Piety, Roman Peace

2 Kaisaros, 8 Kalends October

In Serapion's Townhouse

Serapion had allowed himself the luxury of sleeping late. His footfall on the wooden floors of the second story of the townhouse alerted his slave Parmenon to attend his master. Parmenon ascended the stone staircase at the far corner of the interior courtyard, walked halfway around the second-floor hallway that overlooked the courtyard below, and knocked on the wooden door of his master's bedroom.

"Enter."

Parmenon was a trusted slave who had been put in charge of the affairs of the house and the other domestic slaves two decades ago. He swung the door inward on its iron hinges to find his master dressing by the dim light of the two small apertures high on the tall north wall of the bedroom.

"Good morning, *dominus*. I hope your sleep was restful."

"It was, Parmenon. How long has your mistress been up?"

"She has been awake for some time, *dominus*, and is at present giving instructions to Kreusa and Eirene concerning the day's purchases and meals."

Parmenon stepped forward to adjust the folds in his master's cloak.

Serapion smiled. "You are more reliable than any mirror, Parmenon."

"Thank you, *dominus*. I've set your breakfast in the courtyard, if you wish to take it there."

"That will be fine. And bring Euplus to me there."

"Yes, *dominus*. I have already reprimanded him for displeasing you yesterday and withheld his supper rations last night."

"Your efforts are appreciated, but he'll not get off that easily."

"I'll bring the strap as well, *dominus*," Parmenon said as he bowed slightly, turned, and walked off to carry out his master's wishes.

"And bring my son, if he is still about," Serapion called out after him.

Serapion stepped into the corridor and breathed in the fresher air that the open courtyard afforded. He descended the steps and crossed into the courtyard proper. There, on a small table, sat a serving tray with figs, olives, nuts, some freshly baked bread, still steaming, and a goblet of well-diluted wine. He sat down on a stone bench, furnished with cushions, and began chewing on a fig.

Parmenon emerged from the direction of the house's atrium and front entrance, followed by a teenage boy wearing a simple tunic, his eyes fixed on the ground in front of him. Behind both came a young man in his early twenties sporting a well-bleached tunic of finer linen. The three fanned out before Serapion.

"Good morning, Father," said the young man. "I hope you are well."

"Good morning, Hippicus. Yes, well indeed, after a good sleep."

Serapion rose and stood in front of the teenager, who lowered his head further.

"And what have you to say for yourself, Euplus?"

Figure 2.1. A view of several rooms off a central courtyard in one of the Terrace Houses.

"I am sorry to have displeased you, *dominus*," the slave offered meekly.

"Displeased me?" Serapion's voice was cold. "You need to reserve that verb for instances when you obey me and do a mediocre job of it. You *disobeyed* me. You *defied* me."

Euplus nodded slightly to acknowledge the charge and raised his eyes to look at his master straight on.

"I try to fulfill diligently every command of yours," Euplus said evenly. "But how can I obey when you order me to disobey God? Surely you cannot wish me to lose my own soul!"

"Soul?" snorted Serapion. "You are merely a *body*—a fact of which I intend to remind you."

Serapion looked to Parmenon, who stepped forward, pushed Euplus to the ground by the shoulders, and pulled Euplus's tunic up over his head, exposing his back. Parmenon extended his arm, offering a thick leather strap to his master.

"No. Give it to Hippicus," Serapion barked. "Son, you need to learn how to deal with defiant slaves. You can start today."

Hippicus hesitated, then obediently wrapped the bottom end of the strap around his palm twice, raised his arm, and brought the strap down across Euplus's back with an unimpressive thud.

"No, son. You need to bring it down on his back like you were going to strike all the way to the ground with it. Remember, a proper beating today can save an asset from a cross or an arena tomorrow."

Serapion watched as Hippicus tightened his grip and brought his arm down more forcefully, producing a crack against the slave's bare skin that echoed off the stone walls of the courtyard. Euplus let out a cry fueled by equal parts of pain and surprise that his young master had so quickly perfected the skill.

"*That's* it," said Serapion as he sat back down and took the goblet of wine in his hand. "Keep doing it, just like that."

Hippicus looked down at the welt that was beginning to rise on the slave's back and brought the strap down on Euplus's back again with equivalent effect.

Isidora came rushing into the courtyard at the second cry, followed closely by Kreusa and Eirene.

"What's all this, husband?"

"Good morning, Isidora. You arose so quietly this morning I didn't even stir. This slave just needed to be reminded"—he spoke now more for Euplus's benefit—"that a master's orders are not options to be weighed but mandates to be obeyed."

Serapion looked expectantly at Hippicus, who obliged his father with a third crack.

"Euplus is an excellent slave, husband. He serves us well; he is deferential and reliable. Surely you can forgive him this one transgression—a transgression of conscience—in light of his exemplary conduct otherwise."

Isidora winced as a fourth crack resounded behind her, followed instantly by a muffled cry.

"*He's* a slave who disobeyed his master. But now suddenly *I'm* the problem here? *I'm* the one in the wrong? Where's your head, woman?"

A fifth crack of the strap underscored Serapion's question.

"He will go as *I* direct in everything, and not dishonor my wishes in *anything*." Serapion settled sullenly into the cushions. "And neither will *you*."

"It's alright, *domina*," Euplus said unexpectedly. "It finds favor with God when we suffer unjustly because we are mindful of his commands. I gladly submit to this as the price of honoring him."

Serapion could not believe his ears. Hippicus raised his arm again, but his father waved him off and leapt from his bench.

"You gladly *submit*? As if you had some *choice* in the matter? *Unjustly*? As if it's a slave's place to judge his master?"

Serapion took the leather strap from his son, doubled it on itself, and lay into Euplus with a furious volley of continuous blows, alternating between backhand and forehand as he brought the strap down upon the growing grid of welts. Euplus could barely take in enough breaths to cry out. At last Serapion handed the strap to Parmenon, put his sandal on Euplus's posterior, and shoved him forward onto the ground.

"When I tell you that the whole household is going to participate in a sacred procession, that includes *you*. Disobedience is not an option. Now get on with your duties. Do *not* test me again."

Euplus put the tunic back over his head, wincing as it rubbed against his welts, then scampered forward onto his feet and ran back to finish sweeping the atrium, his legs quivering beneath him from the shock of the beating. Parmenon followed to make sure Euplus could still function properly, waving Kreusa and Eirene back to their tasks as he went.

Serapion sat back down, angrier now with his slave than he had been the morning before.

"What god teaches slaves to disobey and judge their masters?" he snorted. "Not a god who is a friend of the order of the world—some rebel, chaos god perhaps."

Isidora was still holding her hands folded in front of her mouth, her eyes wide.

"I blame Amyntas," Serapion added after a moment. "His godless superstition has infected my household."

He thought once again about the strange songs that rose into the night air from Amyntas's courtyard on the night of every first day of the week. He imagined Euplus listening, perhaps even sneaking out at night to join the illicit gathering and drinking in its subversive doctrines.

"By your leave, father," Hippicus said, interrupting his thoughts, "I'll go to the gymnasium now and see what help I can give to the trainers."

"Yes, by all means, Hippicus," Serapion said. "Have an enjoyable time."

Hippicus began to leave, but his father's voice recalled him.

"I'm proud of you, son. You did well. It's not always easy to remember, let alone to enforce, the essential differences between master and slave."

"Thank you, father," Hippicus said, smiling as he left.

Serapion turned back to his breakfast.

"I can remember—I was no more than ten at the time—how I watched thousands of citizens streaming down that street toward the theater," he said to his wife, gesticulating in the direction of the front of his townhouse, as if he could see through the plastered stone. "When this Christ-cult first came to Ephesus, there was such an outcry against it. People understood then what a threat it represented to proper piety."

Isidora had regained her composure and sat down beside her husband.

"We've grown too lax, too careless. And so the infection spreads. Well, that all has to stop, and we can start with Amyntas. It's not right. A man with no respect for the gods does not deserve this city's respect. Ambition without piety—it's not honest. Well, last night's dinner conversation gave me an idea."

Serapion rose from the bench with a fresh determination. "Amyntas will take an interest once again in our city's gods, or he will show the city just how impious he has become."

THE HARBOR OF EPHESUS

"We won't have any day laborers available for you to hire until tomorrow," the harbor master said to the fifty-five-year-old man standing before him. "Every last available hand of mine has been put to work offloading *that* ship's cargo"—here he pointed—"and moving it to the construction site."

Titus Flavius Zeuxis followed the direction of the harbor-master's index finger across the harbor toward a sixty-foot-long hulk of red granite, hewn into the rough form of a column. It was being slowly rolled off a specially designed freighter on the massive carts to which it had been strapped since it left its quarry in Egypt. Zeuxis could see the ridges of two more like it still sitting on board.

"The ship arrived yesterday evening, and we've had to give it priority. There are two more ships bound from Alexandria behind it. All these columns are for the new gymnasium and bath complex a short way up Harbor Street."

Zeuxis sighed. "I'll take my chances finding some more hands in the forum. In the meanwhile, I don't want to be asked to moor offshore."

"Of course, of course. Leave your ship at the dock till you offload."

Zeuxis signaled his appreciation with a nod. The harbormaster descended from Zeuxis's ship by the gangway and moved on to another recently arrived boat. Zeuxis rolled his eyes in his sun- and salt-weathered face and turned to his waiting crew.

"You all may be in for a long day. Start bringing everything up from below decks. I'll try to scare up some extra hands. If I'm able to send anyone back here, I want one of *you* working with one of *them* at all times—no cargo walking off this time."

Zeuxis threw off his outer cloak, went into his cabin to retrieve the cargo manifest and a wooden box, and walked back down the gangway onto the great stone and cement quay. He followed its semicircular course past the warehouses where grain from the lands south of the Black Sea were stored, awaiting transport to Rome. Moving like two great lines of ants, imperial slaves carried large sacks of the grain over their shoulders from the warehouse to a ship moored alongside the quay—one of the last they would load before the end of the sailing season—and returned again for the next sack, and the next.

Just beyond, another ship—significantly larger than his own—was being stocked with great slabs of marble, some of greenish hue, some of pink, some of the more standard white, all cut from the imperial quarries operating throughout the province of Asia. A group of merchants and sailors was making offerings of incense, grain, and wine at a small shrine to Hermes and the twins, Castor and Pollux, their patron deities. His forward progress was halted as drivers led herds of sheep and swine across the quay onto another ship, already stocked with ample fodder to sustain them on their voyage and keep them fresh for the meat markets of Rome.

Zeuxis came at last to the great triple-arched gate that opened onto the broad street leading to the commercial heart of the city. He made his way to the customs office on the seaward side of the

TITUS FLAVIUS ZEUXIS

Outside the northern gate of Hierapolis stands an impressive mausoleum erected in the late first century AD bearing this inscription: "[T. Fla]vius Zeuxis, merchant,[a] having sailed beyond the Cape of Malea to Italy seventy-two times, prepared this tomb for himself and for his children, Flavius Theodorus and Flavius Theudas, and for whomever they might wish to inter with them."

The name Flavius, carried by Zeuxis and his offspring, likely indicates that either he or his father was a freedman of the Flavian household. Imperial freedmen were often well positioned to prosper both before and after manumission.

We do not know what the historical Zeuxis carried in his ship. Given his location in Hierapolis, he may have been a shipper of the textile products for which his native city and its neighbors, Colossae and Laodicea, were known. Ephesus would have been the port closest to him, though it is not impossible that he made the better, if less convenient, harbor at Smyrna his principal port.

Figure 2.2. The mausoleum of Titus Flavius Zeuxis outside the northern gate of the city of Hierapolis.

---

[a]Possibly "an industrious man" (*ergastēs*).

gate that dealt with imports and politely took his place at the end of a short queue, taking care to catch the eye of the chief customs officer and wave his salutations. The slightly built man squinted from across the room to bring Zeuxis's face into focus.

"Ah, Zeuxis! Back from Rome again!"

"Indeed, with life and cargo intact, may God be praised."

"Let me finish up with this gentleman and I'll come right out."

Zeuxis nodded appreciatively, stepped out of the line, and sat down on a bench outside the office. He watched a group of four soldiers loitering about beside the gate, a well-placed, token reminder of Roman law and Roman enforcement, stationed here in case the customs assessors needed muscle. Within minutes the officer emerged.

"What's the news from Rome?"

"No firsthand information this time, Nicephorus. I traveled no farther than the port of Ostia, wanting to return while the sea was still reliable. However, I gathered a few small tidbits for you while I was there."

"Don't keep me in suspense, Zeuxis. Tell me!"

"First off, Domitian completed his manmade lake on the far shore of the Tiber from Rome and staged naval battles there for public entertainment."

"Only in Rome could one see such marvels," Nicephorus said admiringly, "but I've heard this news already."

"Have you also heard, then, that the emperor conducted a trial of a Vestal Virgin accused of serial fornication? She was sentenced to be buried alive in an underground vault and her various lovers beaten to death by the lictors with their rods in the principal forum."

"Rightly so! Such desecration of Vesta's sacred vessels cannot go unpunished."

"Ah! Most important!" Zeuxis said as if just remembering. "The revolt led by Lucius Antonius Saturninus, that rebel general of the legions in Germany, has been decisively suppressed. Domitian had Saturninus's corpse carried back to Rome so that his severed head could be displayed on the speaker's platform in the forum."

"And may the gods do likewise to all who oppose our lord and god! Thank you, Zeuxis. I shall miss hearing of the goings-on in the world while all of you seafarers hibernate on land these next five months."

"But I have not only collected news for you, Nicephorus."

Zeuxis held out the wooden box that he had been carrying, unfastened the catch, and opened the lid.

"Oh!" Nicephorus said with transparent delight. "These are exquisite!"

Zeuxis looked down himself at the two goblets fashioned from blue glass, nestled in their bed of sawdust and chaff that had kept them safe during their two-week sea voyage from Italy, before closing the box and handing it to his friend.

"Perhaps you and your wife can drink to my health and good fortune tonight."

"Indeed we will, Zeuxis, and to your long life."

Zeuxis presented Nicephorus with the tablet containing his cargo manifest.

"Ah, very good, Zeuxis. I'll tally the amount due by this afternoon. You can start unloading your cargo in the meanwhile. We can forgo the inspection, as usual."

Nicephorus handed Zeuxis a small bill of customs indicating that he had been cleared, which Zeuxis placed in the leather purse he wore slung around his shoulder.

"Thank you, as always, for your accommodating spirit, Nicephorus."

"It's the least I can do for a friend such as yourself."

Zeuxis smiled as he walked through the triple-arched gate and onto the road paved with great white flagstones, fully ten meters wide, that led into the city. Making friends with the customs officer and renewing that friendship with regular gifts had greatly facilitated his comings and goings through the port of Ephesus—and the movement of *un*declared cargoes.

He had not walked fifty paces before he saw the bath and gymnasium complex to the left, rising above the storerooms and shops that lined the street. Two more of the monolithic red-granite columns had been erected since he had last walked down this road, it having taken the masons that long to finish the smoothing and polishing of the rough surfaces.[1] The brickwork of the bathhouses seemed to rise higher than before, though it would no doubt require two years at least to cover the brick core with marble and do the finish work.

Zeuxis weaved his way around the slower-moving carts hauling a variety of cargoes from the docks toward the commercial agora, careful not to step into the traffic of carts transporting cargoes toward the docks. He saw a pair of sailors he knew playing a game on a board carved into a large stone off to the side of the road.

"It's still morning, men!" he said, chiding them in a playful tone. "Time for more productive work than pushing tiles around on a stone!"

"Just passing the time between the hours when the brothels close," one sailor retorted slyly, "and the taverns open."

"Come to town with some money, then? No need for any more to spend at the brothels and taverns? Getting the better class of wine and the better class of women?"

"I don't need *better* wine—or better women for that matter," replied the sailor, "but I wouldn't mind *more* of each. Are you offering work?"

---

[1] A number of these can still be seen in Hagia Sophia in Istanbul, Turkey. Several of these massive columns were removed from Ephesus and repurposed to adorn the new, grand basilica.

Figure 2.3. Some of the columns once adorning the Harbor Baths in Ephesus, repurposed for the Hagia Sophia Church in Constantinople (Istanbul).

"Yes—now that I know my money will be spent for a good cause. My crew could use help offloading our cargo and moving it to my warehouse. A denarius each for the rest of the day." Zeuxis scrutinized the second sailor's position on the board. "If you work better than you play the game of Twelve."

"As long as we're off by the eleventh hour, that sounds all right."

"Good, then. Head to the left on the quay past the granaries and look for the ship called the *Leviathan*. My crew is already working there. You'll need to get there before the other people I just hired, because I'm only paying the first six men."

Zeuxis continued walking, smirking to himself as the two sailors hastily gathered up their playing pieces and hurried down toward the great gate. He looked ahead to the great theater rising above the lower city at the head of Harbor Street. Over the top of the three-story stage building he could see people scattered about in the uppermost tiers of the semi-circular seating, presumably watching a drama in progress. As he passed the warehouse within which he rented storage space, he saw a cargo of a different sort being moved down toward the harbor—thirty or so men in shackles, chained to one another at the neck.

Figure 2.4. A view of the main street leading from the theater to the harbor in Ephesus.

His good humor evaporated instantly, as he was transported back twenty-some years to his native Caesarea. Then an imperial slave himself, attached to the praetorium, his skills as a pilot were put to work transporting hundreds upon hundreds of Galilean prisoners of war—rebels and innocents alike—to Rome to be sold in the slave markets. He remembered many of the faces that stared at him during those voyages, some accusing him that he would participate in the degradation of his countrymen, some pleading with their eyes for him to do what he simply could not.

He halted for a moment to compose himself, to move again in his mind through the steps that separated him from the horror of those years. Vespasian, upon his accession to imperial power, had unexpectedly manumitted him, together with his family, for his unflinching service during the war. Zeuxis had remained in Judea in the service of Vespasian's son Titus, whom Vespasian had left behind to finish putting down the revolt. Thankfully, Zeuxis's duties mainly involved bringing supplies to Caesarea for Titus's troops, as the slave traders had by then gathered en masse like so many buzzards around sick animals and were handling the transportation of their purchases themselves. When Titus had gained the victory a year later, Zeuxis asked to be allowed to take his leave. Titus understood—indeed, for a general whose enemy had opposed him to the bitter end, he had been surprisingly sympathetic toward Zeuxis, and had sent him and his family away with a gift so generous that it allowed Zeuxis to establish himself in business in Asia with relative ease.

Zeuxis inhaled deeply and moved on, arriving at the head of Harbor Street. To his left, the sons of the Ephesian elite were practicing wrestling moves in the exercise court of the old gymnasium, soon to abandon their activity for a bath and late-morning lessons in the lecture halls and porticoes of the facility.

To his right, at last, was the connecting road that led into the great commercial forum. He emerged through a gate into a vast square space, greater than one hundred meters on every side, bordered by a double-aisled covered portico. Running along the backs of three of the four porticoes were sixty permanent barrel-vaulted shops. A second story over the south and east porticoes provided more storefronts for rent.

Zeuxis stepped out into the open square and made his way through the carts and kiosks where day vendors made their wares available. He lingered over some of the food carts, not yet having had his morning meal, but pressed on across the square toward his objective. At the center of the square stood a statue of the emperor Claudius riding on a horse, today overseeing the sale of live animals held in pens around the statue base. Weaving through a series of pottery vendors' kiosks, he came to a larger pen created by portable wooden barriers bearing the name of Hermotimus, the *agoranomos*, the official in charge of enforcing fair weights and practices in the forum. Zeuxis awkwardly made his way around the perimeter of this space, squeezing between the fence and vendors' carts, until he could leave the fence behind him and enter the west portico across from a particular business that had expanded sufficiently to fill four adjacent storefronts. Two men were standing in front of a table loaded with fine woolen garments.

"Six denarii per piece," offered a Greek buyer. "That's the price at which I sell them in Colophon."

"Seven," the olive-skinned Italian merchant offered nonchalantly.

"If you were not here, I would be buying these for *five* denarii apiece!" the Greek buyer shouted.

The Italian merchant turned away from his competition and smiled at the sturdily built man in his late thirties standing behind the table.

Figure 2.5. A view of two of the columned porches surrounding the commercial forum.

Figure 2.6. A view of the commercial forum and the street leading to the great theater, taken from the terrace houses.

"Then it is fortunate for you, Demetrius, that I *am* here today. The whole lot, seven denarii apiece, then?"

Demetrius rubbed his hand against his closely cropped black hair and finally nodded.

"I'm sorry, Timon," Demetrius said genuinely. "But—the highest bidder and all."

"And no Asian wool for the people of *Asian* Colophon? You know that it's hard to get goods there, with every city sending its products to Ephesus and Smyrna to be exported."

"Come back early next week. I'll have more coming in from Laodicea and Hierapolis by then."

"I'll take those too," said the Italian evenly.

"Are you also going to buy up all the sheep and goats as well?" Timon asked, not hiding his exasperation.

"I have orders to fill, Greek, and *I* do not disappoint my buyers— not when they'll pay me twice *whatever* I need to pay here. I'm heading to Miletus's market tomorrow for the fine wool of that city. I'll give you *eight* denarii apiece for next week's stock when it arrives, for the convenience of making an advance purchase. And while I'm here, all the bolts you have available of that marvelous rain-resistant weave you clever Asians are able to fashion."

Timon stalked away before Demetrius could say anything. Zeuxis watched patiently as Demetrius finished the tally for the Italian buyer, received an impressive pile of gold aurei,[2] and brought out several bolts of wool for the Italian's slaves to carry off along with the sixty garments.

"The Romans just love the soft wool of the Lycus Valley," Zeuxis said as he approached Demetrius.

"They'll need it after allowing themselves to be so thoroughly fleeced to acquire it," said Demetrius as he deposited the aurei in a strongbox at the rear of the shop.

---

[2]The Roman aureus was worth twenty-five denarii.

"Oh, don't be at all concerned, Demetrius. Rome will never be able to spend all the wealth it has siphoned off from its provinces."

"Welcome back, Zeuxis."

The two friends embraced and clapped each other on the back.

"Will you dine with us and spend the night in our guest room?"

"Not tonight, Demetrius, thank you. I need to stay with my ship, get its cargo stored, and get my crew working on preparing it for the winter in the morning. Besides, I want to go to the synagogue tonight, as I've arrived on a Sabbath. I like to give thanks to God when I've made it through another sailing season."

"Tomorrow night, then?"

"Yes, that would be perfect. In the meanwhile, I've got some labor issues, as there are no porters available at the docks today."

"I'm sure I can round up some help."

The two were distracted as twenty-some slaves were led in through the gate in the west portico and filed into the space that had been barricaded by the *agoranomos*. Hermotimus himself descended from his office on the second floor of the east portico to supervise the sale, waddling slightly beneath his own girth as he came. A number of men who had been sitting in the shade of the portico awaiting this event made their way to the pen as well. The greater part of the merchants and customers in the immediate vicinity grew quiet, sharing a morbid curiosity concerning the going price of a human being this day.

Before the auction could begin, a man wearing a toga—whom Demetrius recognized as Titus Flavius Montanus—intercepted Hermotimus and spoke into his ear. Hermotimus nodded and entered the pen, surveyed the slaves, and spoke with the dealers, who selected out twenty unremarkable specimens.

"We will begin today's auction with a lot of twenty slaves," Hermotimus announced. "Shall we set the first bid at twenty thousand denarii?"

THE JEWISH COMMUNITY OF EPHESUS

There is very little archaeological evidence for the presence of a Jewish community in Ephesus during the Roman period—merely a handful of inscriptions and pieces of once-personal property (such as clay lamps and a glass vessel) bearing common Jewish iconic decorations (menorahs, shofar, lulav, and etrog).[a] A marble block bearing a carving of a menorah had been incorporated into the steps leading into the library of Celsus (an early-second-century construction). Often described to modern tourists as a sign pointing traveling Jews to a local synagogue, the current placement of this block is more likely the result of the common practice of recycling pieces of ready-cut stone into new buildings. There is, however, ample literary evidence that a significant Jewish presence existed, particularly in Josephus's *Antiquities.* John Hyrcanus II, high priest in Jerusalem, successfully persuaded Rome to grant official exemption from military service first for the Jews in Ephesus who were Roman citizens (14.228) and then, from 43 BC on, to all Jews in Asia (14.225-27).[b] The Jewish community's right to collect the temple tax and transport it from the province to Judea was repeatedly affirmed during the late republican and early imperial periods—showing that it was also challenged by local populations and officials, who probably resented large sums leaving their city to support a temple far away while their local temples were falling into disrepair.[c] The high point in this protective legislation came from Augustus (in a decree to the whole province) and his right-hand man Marcus Agrippa (in a decree specifically sent to Ephesus), who declared that those who violated the Jewish community's collection of offerings would be guilty of temple robbery and denied asylum (*Antiquities* 16.162-68). The Jews' right to assemble and to follow their ancestral customs in general was similarly affirmed. Unfortunately, we lack the kind of evidence that could lead to an estimation of the Jewish population there (for example, approximate amounts of the temple tax paid from Ephesus in a given year).

The book of Acts speaks of a synagogue in Ephesus that Paul frequented for the first three months of his stay there (19:8-10). An inscription mentioning a "ruler of the synagogue" and "elders" in Ephesus confirms the presence of such a meeting place, though it has not been located (favorite options include a number of the spaces in which the artifacts bearing Jewish symbols have been found, but none is certain). Jews such as Alexander (19:33-34) apparently had the right to speak in the popular assembly, but when religious fervor for local religion was high, the Jews could be shouted down with the same fury as was vented toward Paul.

Acts incidentally testifies to the connections the Jews in Ephesus (and all of Roman Asia) felt with their mother city of Jerusalem, for Jews from Asia were present at both great pilgrimage feasts of Pentecost mentioned in the book (2:9; 21:27-29), assuming Paul fulfilled his goal of arriving at Jerusalem in time for Pentecost (20:16). The Jews from Asia took the lead in raising the alarm against Paul in Jerusalem, quite probably Jews from Ephesus in particular, as the presenting cause for their complaint was the presence of the Gentile Ephesian convert Trophimus, whom they recognized as a Gentile, with Paul in Jerusalem (and their assumption that Paul had taken Trophimus with him into the temple's inner courts).

---

[a] Mark Wilson, *Biblical Turkey: A Guide to the Jewish and Christian Sites of Asia Minor* (Istanbul: Ege Yayınları, 2010), 216. The shofar is the hollowed-out horn of a ram used to produce a trumpet-like sound as part of several liturgical observances. The lulav is an unopened frond of the date palm tree, and the etrog a lemon-like fruit, both connected with the celebration of Sukkot (Festival of Booths).

[b] Jerome Murphy-O'Connor, *St. Paul's Ephesus: Texts and Archaeology* (Collegeville, MN: Michael Glazier, 2008), 80. See the more extensive references to the Jews of Ephesus in Josephus, *Antiquities* 14.223-27, 228-29, 230, 234, 238-40, 262-64, 301-13, 314-17; 16.27-65; *Against Apion* 2.39; and the discussion of their rights and protections in Mary Smallwood, *The Jews Under Roman Rule from Pompey to Diocletian*, 2nd ed. (Leiden: Brill, 1981), 138-43.

[c] See further John M. G. Barclay, *Jews in the Mediterranean Diaspora* (Edinburgh: T&T Clark, 1996), 266-69.

"What is this, Hermotimus?" shouted an angry buyer. "I came here for *a* slave, not *twenty* slaves. Who buys twenty slaves in a lot? And I'm supposed to pick from among these three leftovers?"

Montanus stepped forward.

"Please don't be angry, citizen. The city has need of bodies for the games in honor of the divine Domitian next month. We need a lot of fights, a lot of deaths!" Aware of the larger audience, Montanus continued: "Have no fear for the quality of the shows, however—we'll have the professionals work with this lot enough so that they can entertain a little before they die."

Zeuxis and Demetrius could see which slaves in the group understood Greek, as these immediately appeared agitated.

Montanus turned to Hermotimus.

"Twenty thousand denarii."

"Do I hear twenty-five thousand?" asked Hermotimus.

A predictable silence followed.

"No more bids? Sold, then, to Titus Flavius Montanus."

"Look now, citizens!"

Those who had been paying attention to the action in the pen now turned to see the artisan who had stepped forward from his shop and called to them from the portico.

"*There's* the 'Roman peace' for you. Twenty lives snuffed out for an hour's sport!"

"Be quiet, Diodotos," yelled another merchant, a seller of incense and spices. "Crawl back into your hole."

"These slaves will die nobly," Montanus sought to explain, "adorning the celebration of the birthday of a god—whose temple here, I might add, has robbed our rival cities of their claim over us."

"Don't waste your breath, excellency," the incense merchant said to Montanus. "Diodotos here doesn't give a fig for the birthdays of our gods. Why, he was working in his shop here all day yesterday as if the first of the year were just another market day."

Demetrius recalled himself and Zeuxis to the matters at hand for them.

"You said you needed help offloading cargo?"

Demetrius called over two of his stock workers.

"Take our two carts down to the docks and help Zeuxis's crew. He'll show you the ship."

Demetrius returned his attention to Zeuxis.

"I expect my wife here shortly. I'll leave the shop in her care, gather some more hands, and head down to the docks myself as soon as possible."

"Thank you, Demetrius. I'll look for you later."

As Zeuxis clasped his young friend's hand, he thought again about the proposition he intended to make. *Yes*, he thought, *the time and the man are both right for this.*

■　■　■

As Zeuxis turned to lead the stock workers out the west gate and down its secondary road to the harbor, Demetrius turned his attention to Diodotos, concerned about the consequences of his outspokenness . . . once again. He noticed the incense merchant catching Hermotimus's eye and the latter nodding with approval at some unspoken plan and walking away in the other direction. The incense merchant exchanged looks with his two laborers and jerked his head in Diodotos's direction. They rose, approached Diodotos, stood him up, and escorted him out of the forum by the west gate.

Demetrius closed his eyes, shook his head, and prayed quietly for God to watch over God's loudmouthed child.

"Father!"

Demetrius snapped his eyes open to see Theon, his eight-year-old son, running toward him.

"What's this, then? Have you left your beautiful mother un-
chaperoned in this crowd?"

"No, Father," Theon said, laughing at the silliness of the sug-
gestion. "She's right here."

"Well, all right, then," Demetrius said, affirming his son's
manners and taking his wife by the hand.

"And how is it with you this morning, Demetrius?" Olympias
inquired of her husband.

"Good. Italian *negotiatores* continue to buy up our stock,
anxious to get all the goods they can back home before the seas
are closed and their supply cut off until another spring. I do feel
badly for our local buyers, though."

"Their competition will be gone in a month," Olympias reas-
sured him. "They'll be fine."

"Zeuxis is back and needs help offloading his cargo. Can you
and Theon mind the shop for the day? I can leave you Kleon and
Andreas. I've already sent the others to help Zeuxis."

"We can stay. Theon can get us some lunch here."

"Will Chreste be alright at home?"

"She's not at home, actually, but spending the day in
Theophania's workshop."

"Learning the craft," Demetrius nodded, approving. "I won't
be back to the house till dinner. Can you close up the shop?"

"Of course."

"And Zeuxis will be coming to dine and stay with us tomorrow
night."

"Very good, husband."

Demetrius tousled Theon's hair.

"Make sure Mama gets the best price for everything."

"Yes, sir," Theon answered.

Demetrius walked the portico until he had hired two more
day laborers and led them out of the commercial forum through

the gate in the west portico. Demetrius saw Diodotos sitting against a fountain holding a wet cloth to his bloodied face.

"You two go on ahead of me to the harbor," he said to the laborers. "I need to check on something."

As they walked away, Demetrius walked across to the fountain and knelt beside Diodotos.

"The Lord be with you, brother."

"And also with you," Diodotos responded.

"Are you badly hurt?"

"Bruised and bloodied, but nothing broken."

"Violence, it seems, remains the fundamental argument offered by Rome and her supporters."

"They can go on beating down those who speak the truth. They're just storing up for themselves vengeance from the only God. They can strike me dead, if it would mean God's kingdom would come—and God's fury on these idolaters!"

Demetrius was uneasy—not so much because of the convictions Diodotos expressed but because of the lack of concern he expressed for the tragic fate that awaited their neighbors, should they persist in their unwitting rebellion against the one God. He pulled out a denarius from his purse.

"Brother, go close up shop early and have yourself looked at by a doctor. Make sure nothing's broken. And then get yourself a nice meal, and perhaps a relaxing bath."

"Thank you, brother."

Demetrius put his hand reassuringly on the artisan's shoulder, stood up, and took a few steps toward the harbor.

"Have you ever really looked at your money? Each coin tells a story. Each one tells a lie."

Demetrius turned around to see Diodotos holding up the denarius toward him.

"See there, Domitian's little son sitting on top of the world, his arms reaching out to the seven wandering stars. And see there the legend: 'The divine Caesar, son of the emperor Domitian.' What good fortune it is to be born into the imperial family, where a disease can turn a toddler into a 'god'!"

Demetrius nodded in agreement at the absurdity, though he personally understood the grief with which the emperor was trying to cope.

"Go, take care of yourself, brother, and continue to pray for your abusers," he said as he resumed his walk to the harbor. "As long as the Lord tarries, there is hope that they will repent, is there not?"

THE CITY FATHERS CONVENE

Despite having had to cut his time there a bit short, Serapion emerged from the bathhouse more relaxed after his vexing morning. A noticeable exodus of the better class of citizens alerted him that the early-afternoon session of the city council was fast approaching. He walked the short distance to the Basilica Stoa and found himself swept along in the stream of nobles heading for the bouleuterion, situated just behind the center of the basilica. As he ascended one of the stairways leading up through the semicircular seating and found a place in an upper row, he thought to himself once again how the place needed a facelift at the very least, and perhaps a full-scale renovation and expansion. *Another project that present priorities have delayed, probably for decades to come.*

Claudianus, who had been elected as convener for this new year, began calling the assembly to order from his podium on the floor in the midst of the semicircle. Responding to the cue, Aristion emerged from the direction of the Prytaneion carrying a torch, lit from the sacred hearth of the city. All present rose to their feet for the solemn moment. Aristion kindled a fire on a small altar off to one side of the floor. An attendant from the Prytaneion handed him a shallow bowl of incense, which he spread over the fire.

"We give thanks to the gods, to the guardian spirits of Ephesus, to Artemis our protector, and to the divine Domitian for their sustaining graces. May their continued favor and blessing rest upon our assembly and our city."

"May it be so," responded the assembled council members.

Aristion handed the torch and the empty bowl to the attendant. As the latter left, the assembly once again took their seats.

"It gives me great pleasure, honored members of this assembly," Claudianus continued, "to introduce several guests in our midst today."

He gestured to the two men in the center of the front row of seats to stand.

"These are Claudius Aristophanes Aurelianus and Julius Menekleus Diophantes, priests of Asia's Shared Temple of Tiberius, Livia, and the Senate in Smyrna, the former also being my colleague on the provincial council."

Amyntas entered the bouleuterion and attempted to make his way to one of the stairways on the far ends unobserved.

"Caius Flavius Amyntas," intoned Claudianus, "I cannot remember the last time you arrived for a meeting of this assembly on time."

"Your pardon, noble citizens," Amyntas offered from halfway up the staircase. "I'm always trying to accomplish more in a day than is realistic and find myself perpetually late. It is a flaw for which my wife has chided me repeatedly."

A soft ripple of sympathetic laughter ran through the hall, dispelling any tension as Amyntas made his way to an unoccupied seat. Only Serapion was unamused, but he suppressed his urge to glare at the apostate in their midst. Today of all days he had to appear to be Amyntas's friend.

"Very well, then, Amyntas, amend your ways—for your wife's sake, if not for ours."

Claudianus gestured to the man seated beside the priests from Smyrna, who dutifully rose to be acknowledged.

"And this is Nicolaus, son of Strato, of Pergamum, a member of the priesthood of Asia's Shared Temple of Augustus in that city, who graced our own celebrations of the divine Augustus's birthday yesterday morning."

Nicolaus sat down amid the applause that greeted him.

"As you can imagine, gentlemen," Claudianus continued, "the bulk of our business today touches on next month's inauguration of Asia's Shared Temple of the divine Domitian, which we are honored to house. It has become apparent that we will have a good many more official guests from our neighboring cities than can be accommodated in the guest quarters of the Prytaneion or our governor's mansion. I realize that many of you will already be offering hospitality to friends from your own intermural networks planning on being present for the events, but if you would be able to act as hosts for guests of the city, please let Aristion and Montanus know so that their people can plan the more effectively."

Salutaris raised his hand and gave Claudianus an expectant look.

"Ah, yes, Salutaris, thank you for the reminder. We will be providing public feasts for several days next month in connection with the inaugural rites, and we expect record crowds coming out both locally and from throughout the province. The city will need to provide a rather larger quantity of bread, wine, and oil for these feasts. While we all no doubt have contractual obligations already in regard to some portion of our estates' yields, the city would greatly appreciate your directing what portion of your grain, wine, and oil that you can toward our civic storehouses. Since the cost is ultimately being borne by our most noble Aristion, his colleague Montanus, and the college of *neōpoioi* of the Temple of Domitian—and since supplying this temple and all that its rites demand is an honor and obligation that falls to us all as the 'temple warden city of the Ephesians'— it would be appropriate to make these provisions available at the customary rates or even at some substantial discount."

Amyntas raised his hand.

"Yes, Amyntas?"

Amyntas rose to address the assembly.

"For some time now I have been tracking the availability of grain and other staples among the city's poor. We all expect grain prices to rise to their highest point in the late winter and early spring, but in the past three years they've risen beyond the reach of many in our city. Even the coarser barley is barely affordable. The consumption that we anticipate next month will only exacerbate the problem later in the year for these people."

"Though concern for the less fortunate is a sign of a generous spirit," Claudianus said, "this is taking us a bit off topic. But do you have a specific proposal?"

"Yes, I'll come right to it. An easy but hitherto overlooked benefit that we could offer our poorer citizens would be for us to decrease our olive orchards and vineyards by as little as ten percent and devote the recovered land to cultivating grains, which we would make available to local markets rather than export."

Salutaris spoke out above the rising murmur.

"Young man, that's not the kind of benefit that's going to win anyone a statue or even a small inscription somewhere in the corner of a bakery."

The murmuring turned to laughter, encouraging Salutaris to continue. "I, for one, would rather continue to make sufficient money from my estates to provide *lasting* benefits to the city, which will also bring some lasting honor to my name and that of my family. You clearly understand this, since you have undertaken to repair and expand the public fountain at the head of Harbor Street before the theater—and we all honor you for it."

"You are correct that I have begun to seek some ways to give back to our great city," Amyntas admitted, "but we should diversify our benefits as we diversify our investments, even if the rewards are not immediately apparent. And the greatest benefit is one that relieves the greatest need. I think that, come late

---

THE THIRD HORSEMAN AND DOMITIAN'S EDICT

The petition "give us this day our ration of bread" (Mt 6:11//Lk 11:3) took on a special urgency in the ancient Mediterranean, in which there was simply no assurance of a secure and steady supply of grain. Rome undertook herculean efforts to provide this assurance for the residents of the capital city, which often exacerbated the difficulties for other regions. The collection and distribution of grain throughout the Mediterranean, especially Egypt, North Africa, and certain eastern provinces, was orchestrated to ensure that Rome consistently received its designated supply as tribute or at fixed prices.

The two hundred thousand or so families in Rome on the dole, the provision of daily grain, were generally insulated against the vicissitudes of poor or failed harvests in various regions due to insufficient rain, harsh heat, blight, or swarm. In those times of shortfall, therefore, it was the people in the provinces who suffered lack or secured a barely sufficient supply at often grossly inflated prices.[a] Matters became more precarious as increasing amounts of arable land were given no longer

winter, many in our city would find access to bread to be a greater gift than the finest temple. At any rate, I myself have already begun the conversion of a fifth of my own vineyards and olive groves in the countryside."

Quadratus rose to speak without raising his hand.

"The gentleman may not make a popular proposal, but I can tell you all that it is in keeping with our own emperor's thinking on the matter. Domitian himself has been urging his senators in Rome to do this very thing for the sake of ensuring the availability of grain throughout Italy."

---

to the production of grains but to the more lucrative crops of olive trees and grape vines.

Domitian sought to alleviate these problems by issuing an edict in AD 92 that ordered the reduction of the amount of land dedicated to vines and a corresponding increase in grain production. In Italy, Domitian only ordered that no more land be given to vines; in the provinces, vine cultivation was to be cut in half. The landholders of Asia Minor resisted staunchly and were able to win an exemption—an example of the interests of the elite overriding the interests of the masses. In such an environment, the cry of the third horseman of John's Revelation would sound strangely current and plausible: "A quart of wheat for a day's wage and three quarts of barley for a day's wage, and do not hurt the oil and the wine!" (Rev 6:6). A day's wage should typically have been expected to purchase eight quarts of wheat; one quart might be sufficient for a loaf (three loaves if the cheaper fodder of coarse barley were used). The sarcasm of the dreaded rider is evident: "but whatever you do, don't take a hit in oil or wine production!"

---

[a]David Magie, *Roman Rule in Asia Minor* (Princeton, NJ: Princeton University Press, 1950), 580.

Murmurs rippled through the assembly, though it was not clear whether the people were expressing approval or increased concern that even the emperor wanted to cut into the landed gentry's profits.

"Thank you, noble Quadratus," Amyntas said above the rumblings. "I am not proposing policy here, gentlemen. I am merely making a recommendation for each of you to consider and to pursue as your conscience leads. And"—Amyntas paused, hesitating to name all the elephants in the room at once—"while we do need to continue our common practice of releasing our grain in increments throughout the winter season to ensure ongoing availability, we could resist the temptation to increase the price throughout the winter months."

"Ah!" exclaimed Salutaris. "There is a proposal of policy, then. Allow me to make the motion." He placed his left hand on his chest and raised his right hand palm upward in the stance of an orator. "The council and people of the temple-warden city of Ephesus, metropolis of Asia, decree the law of supply and demand to be repealed."

Laughter once again filled the chamber. Serapion allowed himself to join in, motivated more by pleasure at seeing Amyntas embarrassed.

"We might consider," Amyntas said quietly as he resumed his seat, "that the law of love for neighbor has the stronger claim."

"Noble sentiments, Amyntas," Claudianus said with a hint of condescension. "Now if we might return to the agenda, there is the matter of several vacancies remaining in the array of offices connected with our new temple and its cult. Aristion?"

The chief priest–elect rose to conduct this next matter of business.

"Thank you, Claudianus. Most pressing, one of those selected to serve as a *neōpoios*—the noble Lucius Claudius Philometor— has unexpectedly died. Additionally, I think it would be a fine thing for us to select a *chorēgos* who would supply a chorus for the singing of hymns to the divine Domitian, particularly during the rites that will be held every first day of the month in honor of his birth. Both Pergamum and Smyrna provide such adornments for the rites in their provincial temples, and it would be a shame to lag behind them in any respect. As you will recall, we had decided to fill the role of *sebastologos* by competition. That will take place in the theater on the first day of the week, if any of you are interested in attending."

"Do we have nominations, then, for either of these vacancies?" Claudianus asked.

Serapion had been waiting for precisely this moment.

"Noble colleagues, I wish to nominate Caius Flavius Amyntas for the honor of serving among the *neōpoioi*. As the son of a freedman of the Flavian house who flourished because of Vespasian's graces, it would be fitting for him to accept a position that allowed him conspicuously to honor the imperial family. It would be fitting for us to offer such an honor to him as well, as a sign of the city's gratitude for his sponsoring of the renovation of the aforementioned fountain house."

Serapion began to wind the spring of his trap more tightly.

"Now, I've heard some citizens speak ill of Amyntas, saying that he has not shown much interest in piety since he got caught up in the Christ cult."

A wave of murmuring suggested both that this had escaped the notice of many in the assembly and that the association was not a positive one.

"But I, for one," Serapion continued confidently, "give no credence to such slander. After all, the Christ cult boasts some very distinguished and gods-fearing people among its following. In fact, Nicolaus of Pergamum, a priest of Augustus and gentleman beyond reproach, was just sharing last night that he was a devotee

THE STAFF OF THE IMPERIAL CULT

Inscriptions throughout Roman Asia bear witness to a wide array of titles suggestive of the variety of functions people performed in connection with the imperial cult. At the provincial level, the asiarchs appear to have been, among other things, the chief priests of the provincial imperial cult and leading members of the Koinon, the general assembly, of the province of Asia. In connection with either a provincial or a local, civic imperial temple, one finds one or more officiating priests: a *neōkoros*, in this usage a private citizen underwriting the costs of the upkeep of temple and providing various other benefactions; an *agonothete*, a private individual who undertook to underwrite the costs of athletic games and other contests celebrated in honor of the emperor or other members of the imperial family; a *sebastologos*, a person chosen to compose and deliver the hymn to the emperor as to a god (in the cults of the traditional gods, this person would be called the *theologos*, the person who delivers the speech in praise of the god); a number of *neōpoioi*, individuals appointed to undertake various functions and duties on behalf of the temple and cult, organized under an *archineopoios*, their chief; and *hymnōdoi* (singular *hymnōdos*), members of a choir that would sing hymns to the emperor as to a god. In the case of the provincial cults, the costs of the professional choir were sometimes subvented by provincial funds, sometimes by a particular city that would supply the choir. Smyrna, for example, had twenty-four male singers employed for the rites associated with the temple of Tiberius, Livia, and the Senate.[a]

Alongside the public, standard rites associated with the festival calendar of the imperial cult could be found the more personal "imperial mysteries," fashioned after the pattern of other mystery cults in the Greek

East such as the Eleusinian mysteries, centered on Eleusis, west of Athens; the Dionysian mysteries (whose rituals are tantalizingly displayed without explanation in the Villa of the Mysteries in Pompeii); and the local mystery cult of Artemis in Ephesus. The only distinctive official referred to in inscriptions is the *sebastophant*, technically the person who reveals the sacred objects and images associated with the emperor that provided the vehicles for encounter with the god, but probably also the director of the mysteries. Both the larger public cult of the emperor and the more private mysteries, as is true for the cults of other gods as well, were known to employ special effects to make a more vivid impression on the worshipers or initiates, for example in the use of shadows and of lamps to cause the sudden illumination—and thus the *epiphany*—of the image of the emperor.

Figure 2.7. Inscription in Ephesus naming the council of the *neōpoioi*.

One individual, if sufficiently rich and committed, could hold multiple titles simultaneously. For example, there is an inscription associating Titus Flavius Montanus with the titles "high priest of Asia's shared temple in Ephesus, *sebastophant*, and *agonothete* for life" from some point between AD 90 and 112.[b]

---

[a]Steven Friesen, *Imperial Cults and the Apocalypse of John: Reading Revelation in the Ruins* (Oxford: Oxford University Press, 2001), 107.
[b]Friesen, *Imperial Cults*, 114.

of this cult. I could never believe Amyntas to be less pious toward our city's gods, and so I dismiss these rumors out of hand and recommend Amyntas wholeheartedly for this honor."

"What do you say, Amyntas?" asked Claudianus. "Would you accept this nomination?"

Amyntas rose to his feet. "This nomination for so significant an honor catches me completely by surprise," he admitted quite honestly. "I need to consider my projected incomes and reserves carefully in light of my present commitments to the city. I would be loath to default on such an important trust as this office would confer."

"Indeed, it is not an obligation to shoulder lightly," Claudianus said. "Join us tomorrow morning. Some of us will be giving our distinguished visitors a tour of the new facility, and I have no doubt that seeing the grandeur of the cult center of which you would be a junior officer will help you find your way toward accepting."

"Many thanks, noble Claudianus," Amyntas said as he resumed his seat.

"In any event," Claudianus continued, "we require your decision by the next meeting of this assembly on the sixth of this month, that is, by the fourth day before the Kalends of October, in the *unlikely* event that we need to consider another candidate, so that the Koinon can ratify our selection when it gathers here in Ephesus to meet on the Kalends."[3]

As the assembly progressed through the remainder of the agenda, Serapion kept his eye on Amyntas, enjoying the signs of agitation that broke through the latter's attempts to maintain a calm exterior, congratulating himself on his plan's inevitable success.

---

[3] As the capital of the province of Asia, Ephesus was the place where the provincial *Koinon* assembled annually. See Murphy-O'Connor, *St. Paul's Ephesus*, 84. This was an important venue for communication between the province and Rome.

3

IN THE SHADOW OF THE GODS

3 Kaisaros, 7 Kalends October

ASIA'S SHARED TEMPLE OF THE AUGUSTI IN EPHESUS

Amyntas fastened a thin leather belt at his waist over his linen tunic, draped his mantle over his right shoulder, and folded it again over his left forearm. Once dressed, he exited his second-floor bedchamber and descended a stairway into the courtyard of his townhouse.

"Father? Is it true?"

A boy of thirteen ran across the courtyard to Amyntas.

"Is *what* true, Secundus?"

"Have they asked you to be a priest of the emperor Domitian?"

"Nothing so grand as a priest. A *neōpoios* of the new temple."

"Could you accept such a thing?"

"That is a question that I've yet to answer myself."

A woman in her early thirties entered the courtyard followed by a girl of eleven. Both wore lightly colored garments that reached down to their ankles.

"Good morning, husband."

"Good morning, Chrysanthe," Amyntas said as they grasped each other's forearms.

"Good morning, Father."

"Good morning, Tryphaina."

"Menes! Aspasia!" Chrysanthe called out.

The two household slaves appeared from different sides of the house and entered the courtyard. The six stood in a circle together under the open sky, joined hands, and began to pray aloud together.

"Our Father in heaven, hallowed be your name; your kingdom come; your will be done on earth as in heaven. Give us today our daily bread, and forgive us what we owe, as we also forgive those who owe us. Lead us not into temptation, but rescue us from the Evil One, for the power and the kingdom are yours forever. Amen."

They released one another's hands.

"May God keep us this day in his favor and peace," said Amyntas.

"Amen," responded the others.

As Menes and Aspasia returned to their tasks, Chrysanthe walked Amyntas through the atrium and to the outer door.

"God grant you discernment, husband," she said, reaching up to touch his cheek.

"May God indeed," replied Amyntas.

Smiling at his wife reassuringly, he set out on the narrow walkway that led down the hill beside the townhouses to the Embolos below. A mere two-minute walk up the Embolos brought the great Temple of Domitian fully into view above the shops and colonnades that lined the street. Amyntas seemed to hear the edifice itself proclaiming, though to a very different god, *Yours is the power and the glory!*

At the top of the Embolos, Amyntas turned right into a large plaza before the principal entrance to the new temple. Before him stood a monumental three-story façade, each story with a series of archways running across the entire face. Across the second and third levels, every columnar support between arches bore the life-sized carved relief of a god, some known from the Greek and Roman religion; some local, such as the mother-goddess Cybele and her doomed consort, Attis; some imported from the far reaches of the empire such as Isis and Serapis of Egypt. It was as if the pantheons of every nation had assembled here to bless those who approached to worship at the temple of the living god Domitian.

"Welcome, Caius Flavius Amyntas," intoned Claudianus, who was acting as host for the morning tour. "There must be great excitement in your house today in light of the honor your city proposes to confer upon you."

"Indeed, noble Claudianus, my wife and I could hardly sleep."

"We'll proceed in just a moment," Claudianus said. "We are awaiting our friends from Smyrna who, despite staying in the guest rooms of the Prytaneion not a hundred meters hence, will be the last to gather."

"Allow me to make excuse on their behalf, noble Claudianus," offered Nicolaus. "We were being entertained again quite lavishly last night—and in my Smyrnaean friends' case, well *into* the night, if I could leave it at that."

Amyntas surveyed the group as they chuckled knowingly. Quadratus was present along with Nicolaus; Aristion and Montanus stood at Claudianus's right hand as the most distinguished members of the new temple's personnel. His own neighbor, Serapion, was present as well, returning his gaze with a sly smile. A few other local notables were on hand, all having accepted junior priesthoods and other offices in connection with the new cult temple.

"The plaza in which we're standing," Claudianus was saying, "is not yet complete. The Pollio family has pledged to build a

Figure 3.1. The artificially extended plateau on which the Temple of Domitian once stood.

Figure 3.2. The remains of the grand stairway leading up to the courtyard of the Temple of Domitian.

fountain over there, next to the tomb of the distinguished Gaius Sextus Pollio. The plans include some gorgeous statuary—a scene from the Cyclops episode of the *Odyssey*, I believe. The city has asked them to wait until after next month to begin the project, as we don't want the plaza to look like a construction site for the inauguration."

The two imperial priests from Smyrna rounded the tomb of Pollio and entered the plaza just as Claudianus turned his attention back from the empty space where the fountain would soon be.

"Aurelianus, Diophantes, good morning and welcome," he said. "Now that we are all here, I will ask Aristion, as the chief priest and temple warden of the cult of the Flavian household here in Ephesus and a principal benefactor of the provincial temple, to lead us on our tour of this magnificent complex."

"Thank you, noble Claudianus," Aristion said as he walked a few paces toward the grand façade and turned to face the group. "Gentlemen, it is with great pride that I can welcome you to Asia's Shared Temple of the Augusti in Ephesus. We have spared no expense in our effort to display our province's devotion to the divine Domitian and his household, and to create a sacred space that evokes the gratitude, awe, and loyalty that are his due. The three-story façade that you see before you displays three dozen divinities worshiped throughout the empire, gathered here to show their support for the rule of our emperor and his whole household. They lend their support in nonfigurative ways as well, as this façade also serves as the northern retaining wall for our expansion of the plateau on which the temple sits."

"It was the perfect natural location," Claudianus added, "but not sufficiently large for our grand designs for the complex."

CIVIC PRIDE AND IMPERIAL CULT

Ephesus took great pride in having been awarded the right to host a provincial temple of the imperial cult, whose rites were inaugurated in AD 89/90.[a] Immediately upon being granted this right by the Roman Senate, Ephesus began to refer to its political entities in inscription after inscription as "the council and citizenry of the neokorate city of the Ephesians," making of the title *neōkoros* a claim to status within the province. Pergamum, which had been awarded its neokorate for the cult of Augustus and Roma more than a century before, appears to have followed suit, referring to itself thenceforth as "the council and citizenry of the first-awarded-the-neokorate Pergamenes" in an attempt to reassert its primacy over Ephesus.

In the early second century, Pergamum competed with its sister cities for—and won—the right to host a provincial temple of the cult of Trajan (emperor from AD 98–117). Having built the magnificent Traianeum atop the brow of its acropolis, Pergamum began referring to itself in inscriptions as "the council and citizenry of the twice-*neōkoros* city of the Pergamenes," having definitively established its dominance once again. Ephesus, at a peak of prosperity, was in a position to make a bid for the honor of hosting the provincial temple of the cult of Hadrian, Trajan's successor, building an enormous temple with precincts that

Figure 3.3. An inscription from the gymnasium in Pergamum claiming the city to have been the first to be named *neōkoros* in the province.

dwarfed those of the Flavian temple, thus beginning to style itself "the council and citizenry of the Ephesians, the first and great mother city [*mētropolis*] of Asia and twice-*neōkoros* of the emperors." In the wake of this upset, Pergamum again found a way to best its rival through chronological priority, calling itself "the council and citizenry of the mother city of Asia and first-to-be-twice-*neōkoros* city of the Pergamenes."

While from a certain perspective such civic rivalry may be amusing, the fact that a city's investment in the provincial imperial cult came to stand at the center of these cities' claims to honor and precedence over one another within the province naturally increased their populations' intolerance for factions within the city that were visibly, and perhaps outspokenly, unsupportive of according divine honors to human beings.[b]

[a]Steven Friesen, *Twice Neokoros: Ephesus, Asia and the Cult of the Flavian Imperial Family* (Leiden: Brill, 1993), 41-49.
[b]This is a symptom of the rivalry between cities that had come to characterize the Greek world, about which Dio Chrysostom says, upbraiding the citizens of Nicomedia (in the province of Bithynia, bordering Asia to the north) for their vanity about being named "first": "Such marks of distinction, on which you plume yourselves, not only are objects of utter contempt in the eyes of all persons of discernment, but especially in Rome they excite laughter and, what is still more humiliating, are called 'Greek failings.'" H. Lamar Crosby, trans., *Dio Chrysostom IV: Discourses XXXVII-LX* (Cambridge, MA: Harvard University Press, 1946), *Orations* 38.38.

At the center of the façade stood an archway that disrupted the pattern of all the others, being twice their width and height. Aristion led the group toward this arch and up the grand stairway that it housed. Halfway up was a landing with two stairways, perpendicular to the first, continuing upward in opposite directions. The group emerged in a grand open courtyard atop the plateau. Columned porticoes surrounded the courtyard on three of its sides—the longer, north and south sides and the west side. Around the perimeter of the courtyard were a great number of votive statues of members of the imperial family or of the patron

deities of the cities of Asia that had commissioned these monuments to their loyalty and gratitude—or, at least, their desire to
appear loyal and grateful—to their emperor. Amyntas walked
closer to a statue of Aphrodite to read the dedicatory inscription
on the base below the goddess:

> To the Emperor Domitian Caesar Augustus Germanicus
> during the proconsulship of Marcus Fulvius Gillo. The
> people of the Aphrodisians, friends of Caesar, being free
> and self-governing from the beginning by the grace of the
> Augusti, erect this by their own grace in the shared temple
> of the Augusti that is in Ephesus on account of their piety
> toward the Augusti and their goodwill toward the neo-
> korate city of the Ephesians.[1]

Claudianus noticed Amyntas reading and addressed him quietly.

"Amusing, is it not, how the other cities attempt to assert
some claim to ownership of this great temple, almost begrudging
the fact that it stands here in Ephesus and calling us merely its
'caretaker.' But we have turned *neōkoros* into a title of honor for
which our sister cities now vie themselves."

Aristion led the group toward a chest-high balustrade that ran
along the east side of the courtyard, affording a view of the civic
forum below.

"We decided against a portico on this side so as not to ob-
struct the view of the temple itself from the civic forum below,"
he explained. "We wanted to augment our fellow citizens' sense
that all our proceedings and activity happen in the shadow of
our protecting deities, not least of all the emperor."

Aristion steered them next to a large freestanding structure
in the center of the east side of the courtyard.

---

[1]The original text can be found in Steven Friesen, *Imperial Cults and the Apocalypse of
John: Reading Revelation in the Ruins* (Oxford: Oxford University Press, 2001), 44. The
translation here is my own.

"And this, of course," he said, "is the altar at which the principal sacrifices will be performed."

The altar proper sat atop a large square podium and was surrounded by a colonnade on its north, east, and south sides—every side save the one facing the god's sanctuary. Amyntas looked at the carved reliefs all around its sides. The short ends showed garlanded bulls standing ready to be sacrificed to the new deity. The longer sides were richly decorated with military motifs—shields, swords, helmets, all a tribute to the emperor's military might and conquests in Germania.

Aristion led them westward now from the altar toward the temple proper, standing proudly in the midst of the west half of the courtyard atop a podium reached by a flight of six stairs. Eight tall columns, spaced at three-meter intervals, rose across the front, with two rows of thirteen columns on the two longer sides. As the group drew nearer, two slaves, now the property and perpetual attendants of the temple, opened the great wooden doors of the sanctuary behind the columns. The sunlight poured into the dark cella and fell upon a great canvas sheet, as large as a sail, held aloft at its upper corners by two

Figure 3.4. Part of the decorative base of the altar in the Temple of Domitian.

ropes that passed through loops on the side walls and ran down to the floor, where two other temple slaves held the ropes fast and bore the weight of the screen.

"Not many people, of course, will ever enter the cella itself," Aristion said as he gestured to the group to move forward, "but the divine Domitian invites you, distinguished gentlemen, into his house today."

As they advanced some distance into the cella, Amyntas noticed two large, convex, semicircular shells of highly polished metal mounted on stone blocks three feet high, each placed about twenty feet in front of one of the two lower corners of the screen. Aristion and Montanus each took a small torch from a holder on opposite walls and advanced to one of these blocks. At Aristion's nod, each touched the lamps set within the metal shells with their torches as the slaves released their ropes.

The visitors were immediately confronted, as if by some epiphany, with the image of the emperor Domitian, standing some eight meters high before them, his white marble skin shining like the sun in its noonday strength. Amyntas heard the group draw in a single gasp of awe as if through one mouth. Diophantes of Smyrna was so struck that he fell to his knees in awe before the image, covering his mouth with his hands as if to keep breath in his lungs.

Amyntas felt strangely detached and distanced from the experience. As his eyes adjusted to the brightness of the cult image, he saw that Domitian was wearing his battle armor and holding a spear in his left arm, the shaft resting on the ground at his feet, which were bare in the manner of representations of deities. He felt none of the awe that had struck his peers. Rather, the display had impressed upon him, as nothing had so clearly before, the empty charade in which he was now offered a part—a charade that the Pergamene was somehow able to act out. Here was the emperor as he would no doubt wish to be seen—a towering figure, godlike (no! truly divine!), emanating power and majesty—not merely a man of average height and an increasing paunch. And there in the huddled mass of devotees was the local elite as they would want the emperor, as if through the very eyes of the cult image, to see their city

Figure 3.5. The head and left forearm from a colossal cult image found in the Temple of Domitian.

and their people, imagining the favor they thought that they would find thereby in those sightless eyes.

Aristion and Montanus had given the group several minutes to linger in the presence of the glory of their emperor, then extinguished the lamps. As though some unseen hypnotist had snapped his fingers, their demeanor morphed once again from that of worshipers to that of tourists. Quadratus supported Diophantes by the elbow as the latter rose to his feet again.

"Marvelous, Aristion! Marvelous!" Diophantes exclaimed.

Aurelianus walked over to one of the lamps and examined the metal shell with the curiosity of one who might wish to imitate the technology back home in Smyrna's Temple of Tiberius.

"Montanus deserves the credit," Aristion admitted with uncharacteristic modesty.

"I saw something like this done in a mystery cult once," Montanus explained. "Forgive me that I can't say more," he added with a wry smirk. "It seemed like something that could enhance the experience here."

"This is how we will present the image on the first of next month," Aristion added, "for all who are present in the temple's forecourt to witness."

Aristion gestured toward the open doors of the cella behind them.

"That essentially concludes our tour. The temple's servants will by now have set out a light lunch for us all to enjoy in the north portico, overlooking the plaza below."

As the group walked back across the courtyard toward the north portico, Claudianus positioned himself beside Amyntas.

"What do you think, Amyntas? Is this not a splendid temple with which to associate yourself?"

"Indeed, noble Claudianus," he replied somewhat awkwardly, "this is truly an impressive . . . spectacle." Deciding that avoiding further conversation would be more prudent than lingering here over lunch, he said to the larger group: "I have delayed attending to a pressing matter at home because I did not wish to miss this opportunity to see the new temple, but I really must take my leave without enjoying these refreshments with you."

"Of course, Amyntas," Aristion said. "I'm glad you were able to be with us this morning. We look forward to getting better acquainted with you in the future."

IN THE SHADE OF THE BASILICA STOA

As Amyntas crossed the plaza below the Temple of Domitian, he heard behind him an increasingly loud footfall, as if from a person jogging toward him.

"Amyntas, a word?"

He turned to see Nicolaus coming up beside him. Nicolaus gestured forward, to suggest they walk together. They left the plaza, turned right on the Embolos in the direction of the civic forum, and walked past the Prytaneion with its columns covered with the names of generations of priests. Nicolaus led Amyntas into a courtyard to the left immediately past the Prytaneion and pointed him toward the broad flight of seven steps to their left in the courtyard, at the top of which were small twin temples. In one stood a representation of Artemis, a little more than two meters tall; in the other, a representation of the deified Julius Caesar in the same scale.

"This building says it all for the people of your city, Amyntas. Honor Artemis, honor the emperor, and you'll get along just fine."

Objections flooded Amyntas's mind, but none came to his lips. Nicolaus led him back out of the courtyard and into the cool shade of Pollio's Basilica. The vast hall was fairly empty this morning, as it was not a day for magistrates to hear court cases. As they walked down the side aisle toward the larger-than-life statues of Augustus, Livia, and Tiberius at the far end, Nicolaus began to answer the objections he already knew to stand between Amyntas and thriving in Ephesus.

"I have been a follower of the Christ for decades, Amyntas. I remember the preaching of Paul's coworker Apollos, who came through Pergamum when I was just twenty. But we live in very different times now than they did. We have to adapt."

"Adapt to idolatry, to violating the most fundamental commandment of the one God?"

"A commandment given to Jews, whose observance of that commandment is protected by the decree of the emperors. And since the destruction of their own temple, even the Jews give their two-denarii temple tax to the Temple of Jupiter on the Capitoline Hill in Rome, for its upkeep and operation."

"That subtle subvention doesn't save them from being seen as atheists by the majority around here," Amyntas countered.

"True, but it buys the Jews legal toleration—a toleration that they themselves have made clear does not extend to us. We can't pretend to take shelter under the umbrella of the synagogues any longer—haven't been able to for more than a decade. If they're willing to give to Caesar now what they once gave to God so that they could be free to worship God, why shouldn't we adjust as well?"

Nicolaus selected a bench against the wall of the council chamber, sat down, and patted the stone surface beside him. Amyntas obliged, and the two of them found themselves facing out toward the temple of Dea Roma and the divine Augustus in the civic forum.

"We have to be smarter now. The return of the Christ appears more and more to be an event that we should not count on happening anytime soon. We have to position ourselves to play a much longer game."

Nicolaus paused for a moment and looked straight ahead at the temple that dominated their view.

"There are Christians who have all but ruined themselves in Pergamum by their exclusivism. There was one—Antipas, by name—who even paid the ultimate penalty. When I first knew him, he was enjoying a stable, even enviable life, but he eventually became persona non grata for his outspoken criticism of our neighbors' piety. He ended up murdered in a back street of the city. There was never even an investigation.

"And, of course, there's that preacher who used to go from city to city spreading his venom—no filter whatsoever, no prudence about when to speak and how to get his message across, no savvy about how to present the faith as *good* news for the people in this province."

Nicolaus closed his eyes in an effort to remember.

"John. That's his name. He was fortunate that the proconsul at the time was not disposed to shed blood."

"He was relegated to the island of Patmos," Amyntas added with a tone of sympathy and regret that was absent from Nicolaus's monologue.

Nicolaus turned to look at Amyntas with an unexpected earnestness and urgency.

"Don't make the same mistakes when it's not at all necessary! It is possible to serve Christ *and* flourish here. And it will be better for *all* Christians here if you do. You'll be in a position to help those whose superstitious avoidance of idols makes them pariahs in the city, and you won't be making it harder yourself for the Christians who *want* to get along and get ahead."

Nicolaus relaxed his posture and released Amyntas from his gaze.

"The worship of the emperors has become increasingly important since Vespasian emerged as the victor in the civil wars two decades ago. And the worship of the traditional gods has *always* been important for our neighbors. We have to think about the kind of witness we are bearing to them, the kind of stumbling block we're putting in their way when we treat what is dear and meaningful to them as nothing more than stupid error. They have come to write Christians off as 'atheists,' pure and simple, no better than Epicureans. How can we enter into dialogue with them about religion in the hope of winning them to the worship of the one, true God when they regard us as entirely *godless*?"

Amyntas could no longer contain himself.

"What kind of witness are you bearing when you put on the crown of a priest of Augustus and offer sacrifice to him? How can you serve as a priest of a false god, assisting others to continue in their rebellion against their Creator, and expect to escape judgment when our Lord returns?"

Nicolaus did not seem at all upset by Amyntas's question or the accusations embedded therein. He responded quite patiently.

"I've *been* saved by baptism and by participating in the mysteries of the Lord's Supper. I have taken the Christ's life into my life. And so have you. Our place in eternity is not in doubt for us anymore. Nothing can separate us from the love that God has for us in Christ Jesus. So why should we *not* have the best life now *and* hereafter? And remember the words of the apostle

Paul: 'We know that an idol is nothing.' In their efforts to avoid any involvement with an idol, any taste of an animal that might have been offered to an idol, some Christians give idols more power—and more credence—than they *ever* gave them before they knew Christ."

Amyntas's silence encouraged Nicolaus.

"These idols, these rituals—they have no power to harm you, Amyntas. And my status as a priest of the provincial temple of Augustus and Roma in Pergamum opens doors for witness. On the first of the month I offered a bull to Augustus in the morning and spoke to the Ephesian elite about Christ over dinner."

"Which is how my neighbor, Serapion, knew about you."

"Yes, and it has occurred to me that he used that knowledge to put you in a particularly difficult position. It gives me no pleasure to have served some rival of yours in this way, but you were destined for this dilemma at some point, and I'm glad to be on hand to give you good counsel now that it's come upon you— counsel that a good number of our brothers and sisters in Pergamum and Thyatira have embraced as a way forward for Christ-followers for the long haul."

Nicolaus looked hard into Amyntas's eyes once again and placed a hand on his shoulder.

"The people of this city still see the Christian movement as a threat rather than an option, and all the more now given Ephesus's new place in the limelight as a neokorate city. Serapion is just one of many who will be keen on exposing those who share John's mind, those perhaps too much influenced by him. Tread carefully, Amyntas, and give your neighbors what they need to be able to regard you as an honorable citizen—for your own sake, for the sake of all Christians whose reputation as a group will be affected by the reputation of its more prominent members, and for the sake of your neighbors. The way to reach a person like Serapion is to show him first the piety that he *does* understand, so that you can lead him to the faith he does *not* understand."

Nicolaus rose from the bench with his hand still on Amyntas's shoulder.

"I will pray for you in the days ahead as you wrestle with your decision."

Amyntas was not at all at peace with what he had been hearing, but he sensed that Nicolaus did have his best interests at heart.

"Do you have a place to worship tomorrow on the Lord's day?"

Nicolaus smiled in anticipation of the invitation.

"I do not, Amyntas."

"Please consider yourself welcome to worship with the assembly that meets in my house—the last block of townhouses at the bottom of the Embolos, the second entrance as you walk up the hill."

"It will be my pleasure to worship with you and to bring greetings from the assemblies in Pergamum."

"We gather shortly before sundown," Amyntas said as he rose to take his leave and return to his house to pray through the morning's impressions.

IN THE MERCHANTS' QUARTER

Titus Flavius Zeuxis had spent the whole day with his crew on the *Leviathan*, beginning the wearisome process of preparing it to sit at anchor for the winter months. He had always been slightly uneasy about working on the Sabbath, but there could be no day without work on the open sea, and he had made the decision long ago to trust that the God of Israel would understand. He walked up Harbor Street to the foot of the great theater and stopped to rinse off his face and hands in the water pouring

from the basins of an old fountain house that was being reno-
vated and expanded.

Drying his face and hands in a fold of his cloak, he turned to
the right and walked south down the Cardo Maximus past the
great length of the theater with its stage house on his left. Beyond
this lay a sprawling residential area broken up by taverns, street-
food eateries, and a latrine—*all the necessities of urban life*,
thought Zeuxis. Stretching out opposite and below all of this to
his right was the commercial forum that he had visited the day
before. Some passageways and a great hall gave access from the
Cardo to the second story of the galleries of the porticoes surrounding the commercial forum.

He came to the junction of the Cardo and the Embolos and
paused for a moment by the great square that opened up to his
right. Almost directly in front of him stood a great altar. From
the sculpted frieze around its base, Zeuxis could make out that
it was dedicated to Ephesian Artemis, telling the story of her
birth as the daughter of Zeus and Leto. He looked off to his right
at an arched gate that gave access to a paved road that seemed
to head nowhere save up toward the mountain—the path to the
shrine of Ortygia, the mythical birthplace of the goddess, to
which her devotees traveled every spring on her birthday. He
had seen processions of Artemis coming down the Embolos and
turning on to the Cardo; he had once seen a procession turn in
the direction of Ortygia instead. All at once he felt a rush of
alarm to be standing himself at the place where the three roads
met—at a major junction in the highways on which the worshipers of the false god traveled.

Zeuxis instinctively took a few steps back, as though to move
away from a space toward which the anger of the one God must
surely burn. He looked around him to see whether anyone had
noticed what surely must appear to be erratic behavior, but the

Ephesians walking by paid him no attention. As he continued to survey the square, his eyes lighted upon the great Southern Gate to the commercial forum. He had walked through its triple arches countless times in the course of his dealings here over the years, but he had not looked up before to notice the statues of Augustus, Livia, and another couple standing atop the gate. Nor had he ever looked up to the inscription, whereby the imperial freedmen Mazaios and Mithridates perpetually proclaimed their respect and gratitude to Augustus, "the son of the divine Caesar," and his house.

No, no shelter there from the anger of the God of Israel.

Zeuxis shook his head and, with it, shook off the feelings of foreboding as he turned up the Embolos toward his destination. He took the second alley to the left and continued for some distance past shops on both sides until he came at last to Demetrius's residence. He knocked loudly on the wooden door,

Figure 3.6. The magnificent gate constructed in the southeast corner of the commercial forum.

recessed in a small alcove between two large workshops where by day a good number of women worked some of the wool Demetrius imported from Hierapolis into tunics, cloaks, and other garments. A metal latch clanked heavily as it was disengaged, and the door swung open for him.

"Welcome, Zeuxis. Peace be upon you."

"Thank you, Demetrius. Peace be upon your house."

Zeuxis took a few steps into the house as Demetrius closed the door behind him. Chreste, his twelve-year-old daughter, appeared with a jug of water and a basin, and Theon peeked from behind her with a towel in his hand. Chreste placed the basin on the floor as she knelt down to unlace Zeuxis's sandals. He lifted first one foot, then the other, over the basin as Chreste poured water over them and Theon dried them with the towel.

Demetrius led Zeuxis around a small courtyard to a room with three couches, each only large enough for one person. The two men reclined as Olympias came in bearing a tray laden with two ceramic cups of wine, a basket of bread, a plate of broiled fish, and bowls of olives, bits of cheese, and stewed lentils, which she placed on the table between the couches.

"Welcome to our home," she said to their guest. "I am pleased that you are safe at the close of yet another sailing season."

"My thanks to you, Olympias, for your good wishes and kind hospitality."

"I've prepared the guest room for you."

"Thank you. It will be a pleasure to sleep on land tonight—and far from the noise of sailors."

Olympias turned to leave as Demetrius gestured invitationally to the tray. Zeuxis took a piece of bread, and Demetrius did as well.

"Blessed are you, O Lord our God, King of the cosmos, who brings forth bread from the earth."

"You know more and more of my people's customs," Zeuxis said with a hint of surprise.

"I, too, am a worshiper of the one and only God, Zeuxis. The Lord Jesus ended my alienation from him when he turned me from the idols that surround us."

"Not many of my people would give credit to your Jesus for that, but I, for one, am happy to count you among those who fear God."

The two men ate a few mouthfuls of the food before them and washed it down with a few sips of wine.

"How long have we known each other, Demetrius?"

He thought for a moment about the actual tally.

"Almost twenty years, I believe."

"You were one of the first people in Asia Minor to work alongside me as I was getting established."

"And partnership with you, Zeuxis, has been a major factor in my own success."

"This is why I want to make a proposal to you first, of all people, and I sincerely hope you will accept it."

Demetrius's expression showed his surprise.

"I'm twenty years your senior, Demetrius. Seafaring is becoming more difficult and less pleasant for me each season. I would like to put this part of my business behind me in as few more seasons as possible."

"And your sons, Theudas and Theodorus?"

"Landlubbers, the two of them!" Zeuxis said with a snort. "But I can hardly blame them. You remember how harsh a mistress is the sea! You and I were shipwrecked twice together when we were sailing together back in the day—before you got cold feet yourself."

"Before I *begot* our first child, you mean."

"Fair enough, Demetrius. I'm just glad we wrecked when we were sailing another person's ship and not my own! I've been fortunate in that regard."

"You've got the instincts, Zeuxis. You understand the sea."

"As did *you*, Demetrius. You have the same instincts, and that is why I come to you now."

Zeuxis's demeanor took on a deep earnestness.

"I want you to take over piloting the *Leviathan*."

"The *Leviathan*? How can I leave my own business?"

"You don't have to. You'll be home most of the year. You'll be in port off and on throughout the sailing season. Olympias is a sharp woman; she can keep an eye on the books, and you have more than enough workers under you. If you need an extra pair of hands, I will buy you a pair. Or just take all the woolen products to Rome and shut down in Ephesus for the sailing season. That Italian buyer who offered seven denarii per garment the other day? The buyers in Ostia will give you ten."

"You're really serious."

"Hear me out, Demetrius. My sons, though they are not bound for the sea, have been no less entrepreneurial than their father. Even as our networks in Hierapolis and Laodicea have kept you well supplied here in Ephesus, they have also allowed my sons to develop trade networks in the East—with *Parthia*. The Parthians covet our wool almost as much as the Romans do, and the Parthians have something that the Romans don't—"

Zeuxis paused for a moment to heighten Demetrius's attention.

"—Trade networks with India and Taprobane.[2] Cinnamon sells for three hundred denarii per kilogram in Rome. With our networks we have the capacity now to import *two hundred* kilograms of cinnamon each season, which we receive in trade for the equivalent of ten thousand denarii in wool products. The elites in Rome probably end up getting charged a price fifty times higher than the selling price of cinnamon in Taprobane—and they're either stupid or crazy enough to pay it!"

---

[2] The ancient name for Sri Lanka, the primary source of cinnamon in the Roman period.

AELIUS ARISTIDES ON THE ROMAN IMPERIAL ECONOMY

John paints a picture of the movement of goods and resources flowing from every corner of the world toward and into the one city at the hub of its networks of trade and power:

> The merchants of the earth will wail and lament over [Rome] because no one can be found any longer to buy their wares—wares of gold and silver and precious stone and pearls and linen and purple and silk and scarlet and every scented wood and every ivory vessel and every vessel made from costly wood, and from bronze, and from iron, and from marble, and cinnamon and spice and incense and myrrh and frankincense and wine and oil and fine flour and wheat and livestock and sheep and horses and chariots and bodies, even human lives. (Rev 18:11-13)

The orator and hypochondriac Aelius Aristides, a near-contemporary of John, paints a strikingly similar portrait in the midst of his speech in praise of Rome:

> Around lie the continents far and wide, pouring an endless flow of goods to Rome. There is brought from every land and sea whatever is brought forth by the seasons and is produced by all countries, rivers, lakes, and the skills of Greeks and foreigners. . . . Anyone who wants to behold all these products must either journey through the whole world to see them or else come to this city. . . . One can see so many cargoes from India or if you wish from Arabia . . . that one may surmise that the trees there have been left permanently bare, and that those people must come here to beg for their own goods whenever they need anything! (*To Rome* 11-13)

> The difference in their perspectives is significant. Aelius Aristides appears oblivious to the obvious downside of the Roman economy—the veritable deforestation of countries for their wood and produce and the astounding image of the residents of those foreign lands being forced to come to Rome to "beg" for the produce of their own lands. He, however, is a member of the provincial elite, quite comfortably in bed with Rome and on the receiving end of the profits of this system, and hence gives voice to the public, official story of Rome. John, on the other hand, sees what is left for the non-elites in the provinces after Rome has had her fill—as if Rome could *ever* have her fill (John would say)!—and what the Roman imperial economy has done to the quality of life of those whom the system is not constructed to profit and satisfy.

Demetrius could see where this was going.

"So if I take over the piloting of the *Leviathan*, we are effectively cutting out all the middlemen from your providers in Parthia to the markets of Rome itself."

"Precisely, Demetrius. That's almost fifty thousand denarii each year pure profit for our enterprise."

"But you carry almost entirely grain now."

"And that won't change. It *can't* change. As long as the *Leviathan*'s primary cargo is grain and her primary destination is Rome, the ship is insured against loss by shipwreck both ways."

"Yes, the policy since the emperor Claudius."

"Indeed," Zeuxis continued. "The emperors want to be sure that the people in the capital get all the grain they need, and there's no better incentive out there than the insurance on grain-transport vessels. It's the main reason I got out of the direct trade in textiles when I became the owner of the *Leviathan*: my ship is worth ten times any such cargo. So my trade networks in the area of the Black Sea will keep supplying us with grain. You'll never have to worry about moving the mountains of the stuff: imperial slaves in the harbor handle all the stowage and loading of grain for Rome's supply. You'll just handle the paperwork."

Zeuxis paused for a moment to gauge Demetrius's degree of interest or resistance.

"I've always brought cargoes back from Italy—mostly wines from Tarentum and crates of the *terra sigillata* plates and platters that the elites of Asia want to display on their tables." Zeuxis could not help but shake his head. "It really never ceases to amuse me how the elites in Rome want to furnish their tables with everything from their provinces and how the elites in the provinces want to live like Romans—or, at least, want to *fancy* that they do. We *cannot* lose money in the midst of this madness! But we could stop taking the risk on the return cargo and the bother of dealing with it if you wish, because the profit from a few boxes of dried bark will far outpace a hull full of amphorae."

"What about tolls and customs? How much will they eat into the profits?"

"Not a denarius! Have you never read the customs regulations inscribed on the walls of your own harbor here? 'No one is liable to pay tax for goods carried in service to the people of Rome, nor for goods conveyed for religious purposes.'"[3]

Zeuxis had clearly thought of everything.

"My proposal to you, Demetrius: a tenth share in the profits each year and . . . you may have ownership of the *Leviathan* after fifteen years. You'll be younger than I am now, I'll likely be dead, and," he added with an amused snort, "my sons won't miss a boat they wouldn't ever set foot on!"

---

[3]J. Nelson Kraybill, *Imperial Cult and Commerce in John's Apocalypse* (Sheffield, England: Sheffield Academic, 1996), 66.

Demetrius sat in stunned silence for a moment.

"This a fabulously generous offer, Zeuxis."

"It would be fabulous for *both* our families, and fabulous for me to partner with a man I can trust. Say nothing now. Think about it. You have time. I will be spending the winter between Hierapolis and Parthia, and I am committed to another sailing season at the least."

Olympias returned to the triclinium with a clay pitcher.

"Have you two solved the problems of the empire, or do you require more wine?"

"Actually, I think Zeuxis may have come pretty close," Demetrius said smiling. "But, yes, please."

Chreste and Theon took this opportunity to come into the room.

"Good night, father," Chreste said.

"We have to go to bed now," Theon said with no small disappointment in his voice.

"It's not so bad, Theon," Demetrius responded, tousling his son's hair. "Morning will be here, bringing a whole new day, as soon as you wake up. Let's say our prayer together."

Demetrius looked to Zeuxis, who nodded his consent, and led his two children back into the small courtyard, where Olympias had already stationed herself. They took each other's hands, looked up, and began to pray.

"Our Father, who art in heaven . . ."

4

The Lord's Day

4 Kaisaros, 6 Kalends October

Morning Orisons

In the upstairs guest room, Zeuxis began to stir. The sounds of a heavy door opening and closing brought him to the threshold between sleep and wakefulness. Conversation, muffled by some distance and by the closed door of his room, began to intrude on his consciousness as well.

He turned over, pulled the woolen blanket closer around his neck, and nestled his head more deeply into the pillow. He could feel his body settling heavily into the mattress. Then the sound of singing began to rise up from below.

> *As the sun rises to give its light to the world,*
> *We praise the Son of God, the world's true light . . .*

Zeuxis opened his eyes and looked around the dark room, only faintly illuminated by the early-morning light sneaking in through the spaces around the door.

> *the image of the invisible God, the firstborn over*
>   *all creation,*
> *in whom all things were created—*

things in the heavens and upon the earth,
things visible and invisible,
all things were created through him and for him.

Zeuxis listened more intently to the singing. It seemed to come from two groups of singers, each alternating with the other.

He himself exists prior to all things,
and all things cohere in him.
He himself is the head of the body;
he is the starting point, the firstborn brought forth from
*   the dead,*
in order that he himself might have the first place in
*   all things,*
because all the Fullness was pleased to inhabit him
and to reconcile all things unto Himself through him,
making peace through the blood of his cross.

Zeuxis got up, wrapped his cloak around himself, and gently opened his door to peer down into the small courtyard. He could see half of the people who made up, he presumed, a circle of about a dozen, including Demetrius and Olympias. An older man next to Demetrius began to speak.

"We remember together the words that came to us from Peter, one of our Lord's apostles: 'Beloved, I urge you, as aliens and sojourners, to withdraw from the flesh-born desires that wage war against your soul, maintaining noble conduct among the Gentiles in order that, while they denounce you as evildoers, seeing your good deeds they may glorify God on the day of visitation.' And so we renew our oath together."

Zeuxis listened to the group speaking with one voice.

"We vow never to commit theft or adultery; we vow to be true to our word, even though it should mean loss; we vow to hand over any money deposited with us when requested; we vow to

CHRISTIAN WORSHIP AT THE TURN OF THE FIRST CENTURY AD

In AD 110 or 111, while Pliny was serving as governor of the joined province of Bithynia and Pontus, accusations denouncing certain people as "Christians" were brought to him for prosecution. In the course of his investigation of this "Christian" phenomenon, about which he was hitherto singularly uninformed, he learned that the group's practice consisted of this:

> They were accustomed to assemble at dawn on a fixed day, to sing a hymn antiphonally to Christ as God, and to bind themselves by an oath, not for the commission of some crimes, but to avoid acts of theft, brigandage, and adultery, not to break their word, and not to withhold money deposited with them when asked for it. When these rites were completed, it was their custom to depart, and then to assemble again to take food, which was however common and harmless. (Pliny, *Ep.* 10.96.7)[a]

Pliny diligently confirmed the report by examining two slave women, whom the Christians called "deaconesses," under torture, but learned nothing further or contradictory aside from the details of what he called "a debased and boundless superstition" (10.9.8). Those accused of being Christians could escape prosecution by cursing Christ and offering wine and incense before the images of the emperor Trajan and the traditional gods, which Pliny had brought out for this purpose (10.7.5). Those who persisted in admitting that they were Christians were either executed for their "obstinacy and inflexible stubbornness" or, if they were Roman citizens, remanded to Rome for the emperor's decision (10.7.3-4).

It is thought that some passages in the New Testament reflect the language of early Christian hymns. Among these, Colossians 1:15-20; Philippians 2:5-11; and the hymnic passages of Revelation enjoy pride of place.[b] Paul no doubt echoes the liturgy of the Lord's Supper as he refers to a liturgical tradition that he himself received and passed along (1 Cor 11:23-26 and perhaps 1 Cor 10:16-17). Outside the New Testament, the late-first-century church manual known as the Didache ("Teaching of the Twelve Apostles") provides a more complete liturgy for the celebration of the Lord's Supper (Didache 9-10), including prayers to be spoken over the bread and the cup and a prayer of thanksgiving following the meal.

[a]Quotations are from Pliny the Younger, *Complete Letters*, trans P. G. Walsh, Oxford World Classics (New York: Oxford University Press, 2006).
[b]For a recent survey and close study, see Matthew E. Gordley, *New Testament Christological Hymns: Exploring Texts, Contexts, and Significance* (Downers Grove, IL: InterVarsity Press, 2018).

bring honor to God and to our Lord Jesus Christ, whose name is invoked over us, in all our dealings with the world."

The older man spoke again, initiating an antiphonal recitation between himself and the group that Zeuxis recognized as being culled from the Psalms.

Every day will I bless you,
and praise your name forever and ever.
Grant us, Lord, to be kept this day without sin,
for our trust is in you.
We take refuge in you, Lord;
teach us to do your will,
for you are our God,
and from you flows the spring of life.
In your light we will see light;
extend your mercy over those who know you.

"And now," the old man continued, "let us pray as our Lord has taught us."

"Our Father," they all began together, "who art in heaven . . ."

The same prayer Demetrius and his family offered last night, thought Zeuxis. He closed his eyes and said the "Amen" with the group, finding nothing objectionable in its petitions. Then he shut his door and lay back down on the bed to steal a few more minutes of rest before returning to the *Leviathan* and to the list of tasks that awaited him.

In the Great Theater

The morning's production of Seneca's *Medea* had not drawn the crowds that had flocked in the days before to be amused by the more accessible comedies of Terentius, since Seneca was now well-known for slowing down his dramas with long, moralizing soliloquies. Nevertheless, Aristion, Montanus, and Claudianus had come that morning for a refresher in Roman virtue and applauded the actors for doing the best they could with the somewhat stilted and stodgy material. Claudianus had arranged for some of his slaves to set out a nice luncheon for him and his friends after the theater crowd had left. They were joined at noon by Serapion, Nicolaus, and several others whom Claudianus had invited to take part in judging the contest to determine who would serve as the *sebastologos* on the first day of Apellaios, the birthday of Domitian, the living god, as part of the inaugural rites at the great new temple.

One by one, declaimers from several of the cities of Asia took their place on the elevated stage and delivered their encomia to the small group of notables gathered halfway up the vast cavea of the theater. After two hours, they had narrowed the choice down to two finalists.

Figure 4.1. The great theater of Ephesus, once capable of seating more than twenty thousand people.

"Let's hear Hermogenes of Smyrna again," Claudianus shouted to the manager of the theater below in the orchestra.

Hermogenes rose from his place on the first row of benches and ascended the stage, bearing himself with all the poise of a man who was accustomed to holding audiences captive with his voice. He bowed his head and closed his eyes for a moment, as if to collect himself, and then suddenly and dramatically snapped his eyes open and fixed his gaze on the judges, extending his arms before them with his fingers spread out, as if he were stretching and smoothing out the canvas on which his words would paint their portrait.

> *Seven hundred and twenty-one years since the founding of*
> *the city—*
> *glorious Rome by brave Romulus—*
> *were those adamantine walls shaken to their very*
> *foundations.*

IMPERIAL CULT IN THE
GAMES OF NEAPOLIS

In AD 2, as an act of gratitude toward the emperor Augustus, who had directed substantial imperial aid toward rebuilding the city of Naples (Neapolis) after a devastating earthquake, the city established the Ludi Neapolitana, the Neapolitan Games, patterned after and set to equal the Olympic Games as classically conceived. These games, held essentially every five years, grew in popularity and reputation sufficiently to attract competitors from Greece, Asia Minor, and Egypt. A temple to Augustus and his house (on the site of the modern Duomo subway station) was adorned with marble slabs, on which were inscribed the winners.

A particularly well-preserved section records the results of the games of AD 94. One column names the usual athletic competitions and their victors—boxing, wrestling, the pancration (a no-holds-barred fight), the stadion race, the double-stadion race, the race in armor, and the long-distance race. But a second column features an equal number of events focused not on athletic but poetical, dramatic, and oratorical competitions. Among the victors and events, we find

Quintus Granius Melpon of Nicomedia,
>   for best encomium of the god Augustus;
Hermogenes, son of Apollonius, of Smyrna,
>   for best poem on the same;
Titus Flavius Dionysios of Smyrna,
>   for best encomium of the goddess [Livia] Augusta;
Lucius Titellius Rufus of Smyrna,
>   for best poem on the same;
Titus Flavius Dionysios of Smyrna,
>   for best encomium of the god Claudius;

Gaius Julius Valerianus of Neapolis,

> for best poem on the same;

Titus Flavius Dionysios of Smyrna,

> for best encomium of the god Vespasian;

Marcus Antonius Theophilus of Perinthus,

> for best poem on the same;

Athenagoras, son of Samius, of Pergamum,

> for best encomium on the god Titus;

Emperor Caesar Augustus [Domitian!],

> for best poem on the same.

A sizable portion of the nonathletic events involved hearing and judging poems and speeches praising the divinized imperial pantheon. It is interesting to note how many of the winners of these events in AD 94 came from cities in Asia Minor. Domitian himself competed and, of course, won his event—the poem in praise of his deified brother.

Figure 4.2. Close-up of winners of imperial events from the Neapolitan Games held in AD 94.

Marc Antony, rebel, traitor,
slave to his passions and to their queen,
sailed forth against Augustus, the righteous pillar of the
  empire,
the light that held at bay the darkness of untamed Egypt
  and her magic.
Light prevailed against darkness, as it always must—
may the gods be praised for their providential care!
A full and perfect century later, Eternal Rome's
  eternal foundations
once again were put to the utmost test.
Armies lined up against armies, all of them Roman,
all of them brothers, in fratricidal fury
striking one another down in bloody battle.

"Stop there!" shouted Aristion, holding up his hand to Hermogenes. "'Fratricidal fury'—*that* will never do," Aristion commented to his peers. "It could be heard as a veiled endorsement of the rumor that our glorious emperor dispatched his older brother, the divine Titus, to rise the faster to the throne."

"Good point, Aristion," Claudianus conceded. "Make a note of that," he said to one of his literate slaves, equipped with wax tablet and stylus. "If we go with Hermogenes he'll need to rework that bit." Then, signaling to the orator, he bade him continue.

All seemed lost, the empire on the verge of chaos,
until a new Augustus—his heir and true successor,
not by blood but by filial likeness in virtue and
  excellence—
arose to bring peace and order. . . .

"I like that move," said Nicolaus quietly to the group. "It celebrates the legitimacy of the new dynasty while acknowledging the undeniable break in the family line."

"Indeed, Vespasian would have been pleased by it, since he worked so hard to portray himself as a new Augustus, a restorer of Augustan values and the Augustan peace," Montanus acknowledged. "But we are still only as far as *Vespasian* in this speech!"

"To praise the father is *already* to praise the son," Serapion offered in support of Hermogenes.

> *. . . left after him two lights to enlighten the world*
> *and continue to keep the darkness at bay.*
> *The first light was gentle like the moon,*
> *the serene Titus, pacifier of revolt in the East,*
> *champion of piety and virtue in the West.*
> *But just as the moon, extinguished by the dawn of day,*
> *does not leave the word in darkness,*
> *yielding place to that which is more glorious,*
> *so the full brightness of the sun burst forth upon the world*
> *in the accession of his nobler brother,*
> *our lord and god, the divine Domitian!*

"Stop!" shouted Aristion once again, his hand up to Hermogenes. "Same problem—'extinguished by the dawn of day.' If Domitian is the sun, did he 'snuff out' the moon?"

"Make another note," Claudianus instructed his scribe.

"While we all want to be careful not to give offense by seeming to give credence to, and even to endorse, rumors about our divine emperor," Nicolaus said, "it would also be a mistake to be overly cautious, treating our emperor as though he were a paranoid tyrant and not the magnanimous father of the country that he is."

"Fair point, Nicolaus," Aristion allowed. "Perhaps if we just changed 'extinguished' to 'eclipsed.'"

"And now, gentlemen," Nicolaus continued, "I must take my leave of you at this juncture, as I am expected elsewhere and wish to visit one of your baths beforehand. I know that I am only a guest in your city, but, as I part, I would cast a vote in favor of Hermogenes of Smyrna for the best-crafted encomium celebrating our emperor—and that despite the fact that our other finalist, Athenagoras, is from my home city of Pergamum."

"I am sorry that our guests from Smyrna had to take their leave of us this morning, as it would have been gratifying to them to hear a Pergamene say such a thing," said Claudianus.

"Perhaps if they were here, I would not have thus gratified them," Nicolaus retorted with a sly smirk, causing the others to nod with amusement.

"Where are you dining tonight, Nicolaus?"

"At the house of Caius Flavius Amyntas, actually. And tomorrow I must head back to Pergamum myself, with deep gratitude in my heart for the generous hospitality with which Ephesus in general, and you all in particular, have welcomed me."

"It has been our honor to host a colleague in the province-wide cult of our emperors, Nicolaus," said Claudianus. "Please consider returning next month to join us for a week of celebrations inaugurating our own temple."

"It would be my pleasure, noble Claudianus. I will make every effort."

"And, when you see him," Serapion added, "please remind Amyntas that we anxiously await his answer the day after tomorrow in the city council."

"I will do so, noble Serapion," answered Nicolaus, hiding any hint of his dislike for the man who used civic honors to trap a brother. "And I am certain that Amyntas is immensely grateful to have been deemed worthy of this honor, even if, in the end, he deems himself unequal to the responsibilities. Gentlemen, fare well."

The Assembly in Amyntas's House

Amyntas and his steward, Menes, crossed the atrium at the same time in response to a rapping on the exterior door of the townhouse.

"Menes, Menes," Amyntas said, "tonight you're a brother and not one of my slaves. I'll get the door. "

Menes smiled at his own irrepressible instincts, nodded, and turned back into the inner parts of the house.

Amyntas unlatched and swung the door open.

"Welcome, Nicolaus. I'm glad you were able to accept my invitation."

"My pleasure, Amyntas. I have been looking forward to experiencing how you worship here."

"Please," Amyntas said as he turned and gestured toward the atrium.

The two passed through the atrium and Amyntas's office, the latter beautifully decorated with frescoes of the nine Muses.

Figure 4.3. A close-up of an interior room in one of the Terrace Houses, decorated with frescoes of the nine Muses.

They emerged in a courtyard with columned halls on three sides. Twenty-some people sat on cushions strewn about the halls and open courtyard, conversing with one another about what the past week had brought them. Their attire revealed most of them to be artisans and laborers. Some wore the collars of slaves. Amyntas paused with Nicolaus for a moment to point out two more finely dressed youths—his daughter Tryphaina and son Secundus—sitting in one of the halls with their peers. Everyone was generally oriented toward a man in his sixties, sitting on a cushion and resting against the wall of the courtyard on the one side lacking a columned hall. Amyntas's wife, Crysanthe, was sitting to the elder man's left with an unoccupied cushion on either side of her. Amyntas gestured to the farther one, offering it to Nicolaus, and took his own seat between his wife and the elder. He held up his hand and made eye contact with his sisters and brothers throughout the courtyard, calling them wordlessly to order.

"We are thankful," Amyntas announced, "to have our honored presbyter, Trophimus, among us again after his spending several months tending our sister congregations in the Lycus Valley."

Those who had not already greeted the elder as they arrived made certain to voice their welcome now.

"We also have a guest among us—Nicolaus of Pergamum."

"I bring you greetings," said Nicolaus, "from your brothers and sisters there, and am grateful to our host for the privilege of joining you tonight."

A number of those present greeted Nicolaus, though Amyntas noticed some of them whispering comments to one another instead.

"Welcome, Nicolaus," said Trophimus. "I am glad that you can be with us this evening. Now let us pray." Raising his arms before him, palms upward, he continued, "We thank you, holy Father, for causing your holy name to dwell in our hearts and for the

knowledge, faith, and immortality that you have revealed to us
through your son, Jesus. Glory belongs to you forever and ever."

A unison "Amen" resounded through the courtyard.

"God has given us one another as gifts to strengthen the body,"
Trophimus said. "Does anyone bring a hymn, word of instruction, or other gift from the Spirit this evening?"

A young man in the far corner of the courtyard tentatively
raised his hand.

"Is that you, Burrhus? Yes, please, what do you bring?"

THE VARIETIES OF CHRISTIANITY IN EPHESUS

By the end of the first century, it is likely that Christianity in Ephesus was
highly diverse. This diversity would have resulted largely from the physical limitations on Christians' ability to gather with one another, namely,
the realities of house churches. The spacious townhouse of a wealthy
Christian might afford room for a regular gathering of thirty or so Christians in its "public" areas, such as a large courtyard at the core of the
house's layout. We cannot assume, however, that all house churches
met in affluent homes. An artisan family opening up its workshop and
living space to a Christian group might be able to accommodate ten or a
dozen Christians. We have no numbers for the Christian population in any
city of the Roman world at the close of the first century, but if we were to
assume that the movement had by then very modest success, capturing
just 0.5 percent of the population of Ephesus, we would be looking at
about one thousand to twelve hundred Christians. Assuming an average
size of twenty-five for a house church, that would yield between forty
and forty-eight groups, each meeting more or less consistently together
with its house-church circle. There is no evidence of a rotation and no

"I have been composing a hymn, a special one for just this time of night as we look up into the beauty of the sky illumined by the setting sun."

"Come out into the courtyard so we can all hear you."

Burrhus walked carefully around the cushions of the other brothers and sisters sitting in the peristyle and courtyard and stood beneath the open sky. Raising his eyes to the open space above, he began to sing in a surprisingly strong and pure tone.

---

evidence of larger convocations that might give a sense of unity and begin to develop homogeneity.

In a landmark study of Christianity in Ephesus, Paul Trebilco suggests that by the end of the first century, we might find house churches in Ephesus connected with the Pauline mission and its theology, house churches nurtured by the teachers *opposed* in the Pastoral Epistles, house churches that form the circle of groups addressed by 1 John and nurtured by the traditions of the Gospel of John, house churches made up of the Christians who left the Johannine churches to form their own house churches (those whom the author of 1 John censures), and house churches that might fall even outside these descriptors, whose existence but not location is known from other sources.[a] It was the remarkable achievement of the second century that from this diversity came a greater unity and cohesion that led to the formation of an orthodox Christian identity—a process no doubt (and ironically) helped by the success of a number of heterodox expressions of Christianity against which the others could crystallize.

---

[a]Paul Trebilco, *The Early Christians in Ephesus from Paul to Ignatius* (Grand Rapids: Eerdmans, 2007).

Jesus Christ, most heart-warming light
of the holy radiance of the immortal Father,
heavenly, holy, blessed;
as we come to the setting of the sun,
seeing the vesper light,
we praise God—Father, Son, and holy Spirit—in song.
You are worthy to be praised by joyful voices in all seasons,
Son of God, Life-giver; therefore the whole created order
    gives you glory![1]

When Burrhus had finished, a few of those seated around began quietly to speak praises to God and to his Anointed One. The sound grew louder as others joined in and as each was emboldened by the acclamations of his or her neighbor, until the courtyard was filled and overflowed with the spontaneous confession of the majesty and goodness of the assembly's Lord and God.

When the improvised chorus began to grow quiet, Trophimus spoke again.

"Jesus, the true Son of the only God, is indeed worthy to be praised by joyful voices in all seasons. Thank you, Burrhus, for leading us into adoration. We shall have to hear that hymn again. Does anyone else bring something to share?"

"I have a word," said Diodotos the artisan. "It is a saying of our Lord that I've been carrying in my heart for some time: 'You are privileged indeed when people reproach you and persecute you and say all manner of evil things about you for my sake; rejoice and be glad, because your reward in heaven is great, for in this manner they persecuted the prophets before you.'"

---

[1]While not datable to the first century, this ancient hymn appears to have been a part of Christian liturgy by the early fourth century. It appears in the *Apostolic Constitutions* (8.34) and is referred to as "an ancient hymn" by Basil the Great (*On the Holy Spirit* 29, 73).

"Is there a connection, brother, between this word and those bruises about your face?" asked Trophimus.

Diodotos nodded. Trophimus stood up with some difficulty, on account of his age, walked over to Diodotos, and knelt beside him.

"When one part of the body suffers ill, all parts of the body feel it. Come, you who are close to our brother here, lay your hands—gently—upon him, and let us pray."

Trophimus waited for a few seconds as a group surrounded Diodotos, then began.

"Lord Jesus, you bore mockery, blows, and far worse for us; have regard for your servant Diodotos, who willingly bears abuse for your sake. Keep encouraging him that these light and temporary afflictions are accumulating for him a great weight of glory in your kingdom. Amen."

"Amen," said those around Diodotos.

"Let your kingdom come, Lord," said yet others.

"May all who hate your name, Lord, be cursed," added another.

"Come swiftly, Lord, and take vengeance on your enemies," prayed yet another.

"Now, brothers, we were all by nature children of wrath," Trophimus said. "We must pray to the Lord to change the hearts of those who simply continue to be what we once were."

Trophimus stood up again, this time with the help of Diodotos and another brother seated close by, and returned to his place beside Amyntas and Chrysanthe.

"Do we have other words or revelations to share?"

A middle-aged man raised his hand.

"Yes, Fronto?"

"It is not a word so much as a matter of some concern."

"Please, share."

"It concerns our brother Amyntas."

Trophimus looked to his host to his right with some surprise, but there was no surprise on Amyntas's face.

"I do not go out of my way for town gossip, Amyntas," Fronto explained. "I was sitting in a public latrine yesterday. A group of three men came in together talking, of all things, about you. They said that you had been offered a place among the personnel of the new temple of Domitian, but that is not what concerned me. It is perfectly natural for people of your status to be invited to assume such vanities."

Fronto paused for a moment.

"What concerned me is that they said you had not yet given an answer."

Trophimus spoke over the murmuring that followed, motioning for quiet.

"Brothers, sisters, please. Amyntas, is this true?"

"Yes, Trophimus. I told the city council that I would give them my answer yet two days hence. The invitation caught me completely off-guard."

"You're not *considering* it, are you, Amyntas?" asked Fronto.

"Of course he isn't," Trophimus answered. "Amyntas knows better than to involve himself again in any semblance of idolatry, the foundational sin of the unenlightened Gentiles, don't you, Amyntas?"

"Certainly I would prefer not to," Amyntas finally vocalized after an uncomfortable silence.

"*Prefer* not to?" Trophimus said, suddenly impatient. "'*Flee* from idolatry'—that was the apostle's word to all of us. The antics of those people around their idols, be it Artemis or Augustus or whoever, is honor stolen from our Creator and given to demons!"

Nicolaus could not remain silent any longer.

"Brothers, please. Amyntas needs your support and understanding, not condemnation or further pressure."

The eyes of the congregation were suddenly on the Pergamene.

"A significant honor and opportunity have been set before your brother. And as his stature, visibility, and connections increase, his ability to help all the people in this assembly increases, not to mention the circles that will open up to him for witnessing to Christ."

"Such opportunities," interjected Diodotos, "were also offered to our Lord—by Satan! But Jesus did not bow down to worship the Enemy. Would you suggest Amyntas should?"

"I would suggest that we all need to adapt if our faith is going to survive in the long term. For us to continue to be seen as atheists by the majority helps no one. And it has *ruined* some believers in Pergamum. Do you want to push your brother here down that road? And what if he is forced to relocate for the sake of his own and his family's well-being? Will you, because of a superstitious fear of idols, begrudge yourselves this fine place of assembly?"

"Superstitious fear?" Diodotos retorted indignantly. "Having no part in the worship of idols is the command of the one and only God! And no, I would not wish for Amyntas to play the fool like Esau did, trading in his eternal inheritance for a few decades of greater ease in this life. And I would rather we meet in a cave than in a house maintained by making friends with idols!"

"Idols are nothing!" Nicolaus declared, no longer concealing his disdain for those who thought otherwise. "They're just pieces of stone with no spiritual power for good or for ill. Don't make more of them than they really are, and don't make life more difficult for your own than it needs to be."

"Who *is* this man, Amyntas?" Fronto said, extending more of a challenge than an inquiry. "Who have you brought into this fellowship?"

"I am a Christian like yourselves," Nicolaus declared on his own behalf, "and I want to see our movement flourish rather than be swept further and further into the cracks and crevasses of society."

"You are not a Christian like *us*, Nicolaus of Pergamum," Fronto retorted. "The apostle wrote that 'there are many *so-called* gods in heaven and on earth,' but for true Christians there is only one God, one Lord."

"I have seen the inscriptions honoring Domitian's father, Vespasian, as extravagantly as 'Savior and Benefactor of all humankind' in this province,"[2] added Trophimus. "The worship of these men as gods is an outrageous affront to the true Savior and Benefactor of humanity, our Lord Jesus. Amyntas, I pray that you will not make yourself an enemy of our Lord for the sake of any advantages offered in this present evil age."

"You all are making a terrible mistake, engaging in this unreasonable, all-or-nothing thinking," Nicolaus said. "I know what I'm talking about from experience. I know how my activity as a priest of Augustus in Pergamum has allowed me to spread the seeds of toleration for the whole Christian group there—after *your* kind of thinking led to the pointless death of one of our own."

A stunned silence followed his admission.

"So you're an idolater, then?" Diodotos said, more as an accusation than a question.

"I go through the motions that being respected requires."

"Then you're no follower of Christ!" Fronto declared.

"You haven't kept to the first, most fundamental step of following Christ," Diodotos added in support. "—turning to God from idols, to serve the true and living God, and him *alone*!"

Amyntas held up his hand.

"Enough, brothers. Enough. My wife and I are praying about this decision and seeking God's guidance for us. We would

---

[2]David Magie, *Roman Rule in Asia Minor* (Princeton, NJ: Princeton University Press, 1950), 572.

sincerely hope that you all will pray for us and alongside us, that we will discern his leading clearly."

Fronto and Diodotos were both visibly disturbed that there should be any question, but they held their peace.

"We will indeed pray for you, Amyntas," assured Trophimus, "and we have no doubt that God will settle in your heart what you must do."

Trophimus looked around at the whole assembly and extended his hands to invite them to move on in their worship.

"Let us all prepare our hearts to give thanks to God for what he has done on behalf of his chosen elect in Christ."

"We cannot, revered Trophimus," Fronto said, "with *him* present. The apostle was very clear: we are not to associate with anyone calling himself a brother who is also an idolater."

"We are not even to eat with such a person," Diodotos added, "and certainly not the Lord's Supper, lest we give what is holy to dogs."

Nicolaus stiffened visibly at the insinuation.

"This man is here in my house as my guest," Amyntas objected.

"It is your *house*, Amyntas," replied Trophimus, "but it is the *Lord's* table. These brothers are correct, I'm afraid."

Trophimus rose to his feet again, as if about to perform a solemn act.

"Nicolaus, by joining yourself once more to idols you have cut yourself off from Christ and from the one, true God. You are barred from this fellowship—you are anathema—until and unless you repent and amend your ways. We hand you back over to Satan's realm and power."

"Amen, so may it be," affirmed the greater part of the assembly.

Nicolaus looked incredulously at the elder as the latter simply stood his ground. All eyes were fixed on him in the tense silence that followed, easing only as Nicolaus rose, signaling his acquiescence to leave.

Amyntas was about to object, but Nicolaus forestalled him.

"It's alright, Amyntas. Have no worries on my account—or on yours either. When these backwards yokels banish themselves from your house, you will quickly fill it again with a better class of converts."

Throwing his cloak over his shoulder, Nicolaus strode through the courtyard in the direction of the atrium. Amyntas's steward Menes jumped up instinctively and followed after him, to let him out the door.

Trophimus exhaled heavily with relief and sat down again on his cushion.

"It is an unfortunate thing to expel a brother or sister, but the proverb applies: 'A little leaven makes the whole lump leavened.' Christ our Passover has been sacrificed for us; therefore let us keep the feast—not with old leaven, neither with the leaven of malice and wickedness, but with the unleavened bread of sincerity and truth."

He took a round loaf of bread in his hands and raised it up for all in the peristyle to see.

"The Lord Jesus, on the night in which he was being handed over, took bread. Giving thanks, he broke it and said 'This is my body, for you. Do this to remember me.'"

The assembly responded together with one voice.

"We thank you, our Father, for the life and knowledge that you have revealed to us through your Son Jesus. Glory is yours forever and ever!"

Trophimus broke the loaf in two parts and handed one half to Amyntas and the other to Fronto, who each broke off a piece and handed the larger part to the person next to them. Trophimus took up the ceramic chalice and raised it before the assembly.

"In the same way, after they had eaten, Jesus took the cup, saying, 'This cup is the new covenant in my blood. Do this, as often as you drink, to remember me.'"

Again the assembly responded.

"We thank you, our Father, for the holy vine of David your servant, which you have made known to us through your Son Jesus. Glory is yours forever and ever!"

Trophimus offered the chalice to Amyntas, who, after drinking from it, offered it to Chrysanthe.

Trophimus spoke again.

"Whenever you eat this bread and drink this cup, you are proclaiming the Lord's death—until he comes."

"Our Lord, come!" responded the assembly.

Amyntas rose from his cushion, helped Chyrsanthe to her feet, and left for the kitchen, with Secundus and Tryphaina following behind. They returned with baskets of bread, large plates of fish, olives, and cheese, and small amphorae of wine.

As the air of worship gave way to an air of festivity in the sharing of the common meal, Amyntas could not shake the sense that the lack of love he had witnessed tonight was as egregious a violation of the one God's righteousness as Nicolaus's path of compromise was alleged to be.

5

The Crucible of Faith

5 Kaisaros, 5 Kalends October

In Serapion's Townhouse

Isidora had spent the early morning setting the day's menu with Kreusa and Eirene. After sending them off to the market to procure supplies, she turned her attention to the records and receipts from their agricultural estates, some twenty kilometers northeast of the city. She spread out the documents and her ledger on a wooden table that she had had Parmenon and Euplus carry out to the courtyard, so she could work in the full light the aperture provided.

Around midmorning, Euplus arrived with a straw broom and began to sweep the four covered halls surrounding the courtyard, stopping every so often to gather the debris and place it in a bucket. Isidora found the rhythmic scratching of the broom against the stone more comforting than distracting, a pleasant reminder that she was not alone in the house. She had not noticed that the scratching had stopped half an hour later until Euplus appeared at her table bearing a tray with a cup of water lightly flavored with some rind from a bitter orange and a small bowl of figs and cherries.

"Why, thank you, Euplus," she said, touched by his thoughtfulness.

The slave nodded, picked up his broom, and resumed his sweeping. Isidora watched him for a moment, observing that he was still moving a bit stiffly to avoid provoking his bruised back.

"How are you faring, Euplus?" she asked.

The question was vague, but he understood what she left unspecified.

"Every day is better, *domina*. The unguent you sent through Parmenon was very soothing."

Isidora was silent for a moment, feeling a guilt born of cowardice for not opposing Serapion more insistently three mornings ago.

"I'm worried about you, Euplus. There will be more festivals where my husband will want his whole household to be present. There will be more rites here in our home, and he will be watching for your attendance. He's a deeply pious man, and I don't see him growing softer if you make a habit of defying his wishes."

"May I speak freely, *domina*?"

"Yes, Euplus, of course you may."

"My master's gods have never cared for slaves. Artemis cares for the free citizens of Ephesus and watches over the wealth of the cities and the nobles who have entrusted their riches to her house. She owns many slaves, who spend their lives working in her temple and on her vast estates. Augustus and Rome have been prolific gods in creating slaves out of free persons and ensuring a master's rights over his property, even when that property is a human being like them. And how many slaves like myself have perished for nothing more than an hour's entertainment in honor of Augustus or Claudius or Vespasian?"

He paused for a moment to study Isidora's face, to see whether he had said too much, but her features continued to communicate concern, perhaps now augmented by sorrow.

"But the God of Jesus is very different. He cares so much about slaves that his own Son took the form of a slave, spending his life in service to others, dying the death of a slave, nailed to a *cross*, so that they might live forever—and not just freeborn people, but the slaves as well. God restored his Son Jesus to life on the first day of the week, confirming his promise that no one who follows him will be held by death but will live with him forever."

Euplus fell silent for a moment, aware of having spoken a good deal more in this one morning than he had said to his mistress in the past month. Isidora encouraged him to continue with a question.

"But could you not spare yourself further distress by just going through the motions with us?"

"The God of Jesus is the only God I've encountered as a *living* God. Every other one has just been a cold, lifeless, loveless statue toward me, but this God has let me feel his love, his acceptance, his care. And he doesn't want his people to keep pretending that the other gods are real. I can't make myself a willing party to the lie. If that means I must suffer a beating for doing what is right in the sight of the only God, the God who loved me, I accept it willingly, because that is what Jesus did on my behalf."

He fell silent again and lowered his eyes, waiting to be dismissed. Isidora understood the posture and waved her consent with her hand. He began to walk back to his broom but stopped to add one thing more.

"I'm not angry with my master, *domina*. I love him. I pray that he'll come to know the living God one day. And I will continue to serve him diligently in every matter that my *heavenly* master has not forbidden—and to do more for him than I'm commanded, because Jesus has taught us to do good to all people."

Isidora smiled at Euplus and nodded her acknowledgment of his generous spirit. As he returned to his sweeping, she attempted

Figure 5.1. A floor mosaic from one of the Terrace Houses, featuring Neptune and his bride, Amphititre.

to attend again to the numbers before her, but her mind would not cooperate. She rose from her chair and walked to the small room off the northwest corner of the courtyard and peristyle, where Serapion had, at her request, installed a small shrine to Isis for her personal devotions. She knelt on the cushion before the shrine, held a small piece of aromatic resin over the fire of an oil lamp with a pair of ritual tongs until it began to smolder, and set it on the brick-sized altar before the statuette of the goddess.

She wanted to pray, to rekindle some sense of connection with her goddess, but could not push past the new doubt in her mind that this Egyptian cult would be able to supply what she had already found lacking in the traditional cults all around her.

In the Gymnasium

Secundus sat on a small mat on the marble floor of one of the lecture halls in the gymnasium complex. He and fourteen of his peers were arranged in a semicircle facing their instructor. Demonax, a Greek from Samothrace, looked old enough to Secundus to have known Aristotle and Plato personally. Secundus had only been half present for most of the morning. While Demonax read to them their history lesson from Polybius's accounts of the

Roman Republic, Secundus kept drifting off in his mind to the arguments in his father's house interrupting their worship the night before. He had not fully realized his father's dilemma—and peril—until then.

"Here I've brought with me again our square frame and four identical right triangles," said Demonax, as he reached into a box beside the cushion on which he was sitting and pulled out some wooden pieces. Laying these on the marble floor in front of him, he asked, "Who can re-create for me Pythagoras's proof of his theorem?"

A number of the boys raised their hands.

"Secundus, you've not said much this morning. Let's start with you. Do you remember?"

"I think so, teacher," he said as he uncrossed his legs and moved himself closer to the pieces. Kneeling in front of them, he arranged the four triangles against the inside edges of the frame, the right angle of each against a corner of the frame.

"When the four triangles are arranged like this, their four hypotenuses create a large square in the middle. The area of the square will be the length of the hypotenuse multiplied by itself."

Secundus then made two rectangles out of each pair of triangles, placing one rectangle vertically up against the upper left corner of the frame and the other horizontally against the lower right corner of the frame, such that the rectangles also touched each other at their inside corner.

"The empty space within the frame is in the form of two smaller squares, one larger than the other. The area of each of these can be calculated from the square of the smaller two sides of each triangle. Since the empty space has to remain constant, as the areas of the four triangles remain constant, we can say that the square of the hypotenuse of a right triangle is equal to the sum of the squares of the other two sides."

"Q.E.D.," said Demonax. "Very good, Secundus. Now, on the seventh of Kaisaros, I want each of you to come back with an example of how this theorem might have been used or could yet be put to use to solve some question in our great city."

Demonax retired the pieces to the box. "Enough geometry for one day," he said. "Let's conclude this morning's lessons with some philosophy. We have been talking about the ethical virtue of justice for the past several days. Remind us, Ampelios, of Aristotle's definition of justice."

Ampelios snapped out of his daydream and stammered out, "Justice means giving to each thing what it is entitled in proportion to its worth."

"Not a bad recovery, Ampelios, though we attribute that definition to *Cicero*. Giving to each his or her due starts with proper credit for quotations."

The other students chuckled.

"Nevertheless, Cicero's definition will give us an adequate starting point for our discussion today, in which I want us to focus on the virtue of piety. Why, do you suppose, would some philosophers regard piety as a species of justice and not as a separate virtue?"

After a moment's silence, Proclus, another of the youths in the circle, ventured: "Because piety means giving to the gods their due?"

"Precisely, Proclus," affirmed Demonax. "Piety has been called 'justice in regard to the gods.'"

Serapion's son Hippicus walked into the lecture room and leaned against the wall beside the doorway.

"Good day, Hippicus," said Demonax. "Are you ready for these future citizens of Ephesus already?"

"I am, Master Demonax, but I am also early."

"It's fortuitous that you have come, for we were just beginning to discuss the virtue of piety. Do you all know in what capacity Hippicus's father serves the gods?"

"Yes," said Proclus. "He's one of the priests of Great Artemis."

"Indeed he is, Proclus, and that makes him—and his son here—*experts* on piety. Hippicus," Demonax said, patting the cushion beside him, "tell these young men why piety is such an important virtue."

Hippicus sat down beside his own former teacher.

"First off, I suppose, because we depend on the gods' favor. What anchor for life do we have in the midst of life's storms, if not the gods' goodwill toward us?"

"Excellent, Hippicus. And we give the gods due honor for their majesty and due thanks for all their past favors toward us so that we might reasonably hope that they will remain favorable toward us in our need tomorrow. Why else?"

"Piety ennobles us. The person who reveres the gods will seek to be the most excellent person that he or she can be. And, as Pythagoras said, 'We are at our best when we visit the gods.'"

"I would agree," Demonax said. "When are all of our citizenry better, nobler, and more concerned with decorum than when we are all assembled together before the house of a god? Why else?"

"To maintain the goodwill of our neighbors."

"And why would piety be important to *that* end?"

"If I see a man giving the gods their due and lining himself up with the rest of us imploring the gods' favor on behalf of us all, I think that I can more readily trust him as an honorable man who seeks the common good."

"A fair deduction, Hippicus. And is the inverse also true, that if a person neglects piety he or she will prove untrustworthy?"

"I certainly think so," the young man declared. "Take the Jews in our city, for example. They look after one another well enough but despise our tables and our temples as unclean things. How could I trust such a person to be well-disposed toward me and mine, when they care nothing for the gods?"

Secundus looked puzzled at this and tentatively raised his hand.

"But the Jews care deeply about the divine. They believe that God has given them their law, and they regulate their behavior accordingly. However strange it might seem to us, it is all an expression of piety, is it not?"

"The Jews don't have the first clue about piety," Ampelios said with indignation, "and you're an idiot for suggesting that they do."

"Now, Ampelios," Demonax intervened, "here we examine arguments for their merits, and attacking the proponent of a proposition carries weight only among the uneducated. So take a breath and try again. Why would you not grant that Jews are pious?"

"Because they're atheists."

"How can people who devote themselves to God be *atheists*?" Secundus asked, pointing out the contradiction in terms.

"They might as well be atheists, for they worship one God who forbids them to worship—or even acknowledge—any other god."

"Indeed," Demonax interjected. "They *dis*believe in the gods of all the nations save their own. So with respect to all gods save one, they are atheists. Our noblest writers do not give to their way of life the name of *religio* but rather of *superstitio*. And their superstition comes in several forms, mutating like some pestilent Proteus. In my own lifetime it has showed up anew in followers of some god named *Christos*. These people neither live as Jews, taking on the ropes of that depraved superstition that begins with cutting off the tip of the penis"—Demonax accompanied these words with a gesture, pleased that he had made his students squirm visibly—"nor as Greeks, continuing to give the gods of their fathers and mothers their due."

"One might even say," Hippicus said, looking pointedly at Secundus, "that Christians 'invent new gods and deny the old ones.'"

"Very good, Hippicus," said Demonax. "Do any of you follow his reference?"

The circle of students remained silent.

"Well, then, this sets the agenda for next week's lessons in philosophy," sighed Demonax. "These were the very charges that led to Socrates's condemnation, according to his disciple Plato."

"And if it led to the condemnation of one so wise as Socrates," Hippicus added, "why should it not to the slaves and laborers and nobodies who commit the same sacrileges now?"

"Good heavens, *there's* an ominous note on which to end today's lessons," said Demonax with mock foreboding. "I propose an exercise in the defense of a thesis: 'The person who is pious toward the gods will be just in his dealings with mortals.' Create essays in support and against, using all the elements of the elaboration pattern, which are?"

The students spoke in unison as Demonax held up his hand and pointed to each finger in turn.

"Rationale, opposite, example, analogy, and authority."

"Very good," he said, dismissing them with a wave. "Go, enjoy your activities."

Hippicus rose with them and took charge from this point.

"Go to the *apodyterium*, put your clothes in the cubbies, and get yourselves oiled up. Then come meet me out on the palaestra."

The boys knew their daily routine, but Hippicus always barked out the orders to reinforce that what they were about to do anyway they did at his command.

About ten minutes later, they had all emerged from the rooms of the gymnasium and gathered in the open courtyard at its front. The exercise yard was large—a full seventy by thirty meters—and surrounded on its three outer sides by columned porches. The side adjoining the gymnasium consisted of four broad, raised steps that served both as access to the raised podium of the gymnasium and as modest stadium seating for observing the activities in the palaestra. The stone floor of the palaestra was sunken, to allow for a generous layer of sand covering the whole yard.

After leading the group in a series of stretches, Hippicus said, "We haven't done any training in the way of the pancratium for some time."

The groans of the youths declared this to be one of their least favorite of the martial sports.

"I know, it can be unpleasant—if you're not much good at it," Hippicus said, goading the boys. "Boxing, wrestling, kicking all at once, it's not at all easy."

He paused as if to think for a moment.

"Perhaps if we made it a group match instead of the usual one-on-one? Let's make two teams. Team one, everyone who believes that Artemis and the other gods are great and deserving of our worship. Gather over here if you're on team one. Team two, everyone else. Stay over there."

The boys looked at each other as if it were an absurd way to form teams, since everyone surely would end up on one side. But in a moment, they noticed one youth still standing alone.

"Secundus?" Proclus said, perplexed.

Secundus simply looked down.

"Didn't you all know?" Hippicus asked. "Secundus and his family don't believe in the gods any longer. At least, I know that *I* haven't seen any of them at any of our temples or festivals in ages. Isn't that right, Secundus?"

Secundus still didn't make eye contact with Hippicus but said, "I believe in God."

"Just one, Secundus?" Ampelios asked.

"Don't you believe in Great Artemis and the other gods?" asked another.

"No, Secundus is more like the Jews than like us, aren't you,

Secundus," Hippicus taunted. "Your *phallos* does look a little small, like you had some of it trimmed."

The other boys laughed, making Secundus blush.

"Well, Secundus, you're not in an enviable position, are you? Are you sure you're not a team-one player?" Hippicus paused, challenging Secundus. "No? All right, then. Let's see which team wins at the pancratium."

The other boys were reluctant at first to attack their comrade. Proclus made the first advance against him. Secundus deflected the first punch and grabbed hold of Proclus's foot when he attempted a kick, but Ampelios stepped forward and caught Secundus's cheek with his right fist. Proclus, finding himself released, kicked Secundus in his abdomen.

"Are you all going to leave this fight to your two teammates?" Hippicus said, goading the rest to action. "Let's go, Team Artemis!"

The others moved in and took turns landing blows on Secundus, who could no longer deflect them but only tried to cover his face. After a few minutes, Hippicus blew into a short pipe that emitted a loud, high pitch. The boys halted their onslaught and took a few steps back from Secundus, who was lying in the sand, crying.

"Well, the victory here certainly belongs to the pious," Hippicus declared. "Now head on over to the *xystus* across the way and take a lap around the large field. I'll be over in a few minutes to work you all in your discus and javelin throws."

The boys started jogging off in the direction of the immense exercise yard that had been constructed across from the older gymnasium complex in which they spent their morning. Hippicus walked over to Secundus and knelt down.

"Maybe you should think about being on the right team."

PROCHORUS ARRIVES

Amyntas sat praying in the courtyard of his townhouse.

Lead me, Lord, in your righteousness. Make your path clear before me.

He became aware that he was no longer alone. He opened his eyes to see Chrysanthe standing in the corner of the colonnade opposite him.

"What are you hearing from the Lord, husband?"

"Nothing above the clamor of my own thoughts."

Chrysanthe walked over and sat down next to Amyntas.

"We haven't really talked this through yet ourselves. It might help."

Amyntas nodded.

"What, then, if you accept this 'honor'?"

"I will surprise Serapion, certainly. It will increase our visibility, expand our networks. I'll be rubbing shoulders more frequently with the highest level of the Ephesian elite. And all for the price of promoting the worship of a man as a god."

"Nicolaus of Pergamum found a way to make it work. Could we?"

"'An idol is nothing,' but is there really nothing behind an idol? I find it hard to accept that there's no spiritual power—or spiritual danger—involved. It's also clear after last night where the members of our own assembly stand on the matter." Amyntas grew impatient at his fellow Christians' intolerance. "Most of them don't seem to understand the pressures on people of our station in life."

"They might not, Amyntas, but they do understand the pressure to conform—pressure applied much more directly to Diodotos than to us, as I recall."

Amyntas nodded, remembering the artisan's bruises and swollen features.

"If you decline, then?"

"I simply don't know. No matter what excuse I made, there would be suspicion now that I was refusing because I disapprove of the city's worship, or because I've become an atheist myself."

"Could you prefer someone else to yourself? Turn a refusal into an act of honoring a friend?"

"I've thought about that—even suggesting Serapion himself. But even so the suspicions would remain, no doubt fueled by innuendo and inference."

Amyntas paused to recall a verse from a psalm.

"'The wicked have laid a snare for me . . .'"

"'. . . yet I have not strayed from your commandments,'" added Chrysanthe, finishing the couplet.

A commotion from the direction of the atrium drew their attention. Menes came into the courtyard, leading Secundus, who was trying to control his sobbing. His parents jumped up, and Chrysanthe ran to her son.

"Secundus, are you all right?" she asked urgently, leading him to lie down on a bench. "What happened, son? Who did this?"

Menes brought a basin of water and some cloths. Chrysanthe took a cloth, dipped it in the water, and carefully began to wash

Figure 5.2. The atrium, or entrance courtyard, of one the Terrace Houses, with surrounding rooms.

the blood from her son's face. Eventually Secundus mastered his sobbing sufficiently to tell them about his lesson in piety.

"This will *not* go unanswered," Amyntas declared.

"You'll need a lot of support to go against Serapion," said Chrysanthe.

Frustration flooded in alongside Amyntas's fury. "Support that I won't have after tomorrow if I decline."

Amyntas fell silent as Chrysanthe continued to tend Secundus.

"There is another option," Amyntas said at last. "We could just sell the townhouse, expand the house on our country estate, and live there from the produce of the land and its profits. Retreat, and take Epicurus's advice to 'Live unknown.' At least it would be safe for us all."

Chrysanthe stroked Secundus's hair to soothe him.

"It would deprive our brothers and sisters of their meeting place," Amyntas continued, "but they'll find another. Besides, they're not making this any easier on us."

A rapping at the entrance door interrupted their conversation. A moment later, Menes stepped into the courtyard.

"Diodotos is at the door with a merchant that I recognize to be a brother and another man I have not seen before. Shall I admit them?"

"I'll come myself, Menes," Amyntas said as he rose and followed Menes back through the atrium to the entrance.

"Diodotos, welcome," Amyntas said as Menes opened the door before them.

"Greetings, Amyntas. These men—these *brothers*—want to speak with you."

Amyntas extended his hand to the merchant.

"You I recognize—from the commercial forum, I believe."

The merchant clasped Amyntas's forearm.

"Yes, Amyntas. My name is Demetrius. I'm host to an assembly not far from here, in the neighborhood on the other side of the Embolos. This is Prochorus. He has been with John on Patmos."[1]

Amyntas offered his hand to Prochorus as well.

"I bring greetings from John to you and to the assembly in your house."

Amyntas gestured to the three men, inviting them inside.

"How is John?"

"Well enough," Prochorus answered. "He has freedom on the island and has even been preaching among the locals there. But he spends most of his time in prayer for his brothers and sisters here and listening for God's word. Indeed, that is what has brought me back to the mainland."

"It's a powerful message," Demetrius interjected. "Prochorus shared it with our assembly when we reconvened last night to share the Lord's Supper."

"I think it's a message we need to hear," Diodotos said. "A message *you* need to hear."

"Diodotos has shared with me the choice before you, Amyntas," said Demetrius. "Before you make up your mind, before you give your answer, listen to what John has to say."

---

[1] A certain Prochorus is found briefly in the Acts of the Apostles as one of the seven Hellenistic Jews chosen to serve as deacons administering the daily distribution of food to the poor (widows are particularly mentioned; see Acts 6:1-6). Popular tradition also connects a Prochorus with John, always identified as John the apostle, on Patmos. This appears to have arisen by the fifth century, as seen in the fanciful *Acts of John Attributed to Prochorus* (in *New Testament Apocrypha*, ed. Edgar Hennecke and Wilhelm Schneemelcher [Louisville, KY: Westminster John Knox, 1992], 2:429-35). Prochorus, however, is also always portrayed as a much younger assistant in the iconography of John on Patmos. I think the tradition highly unlikely to be reliable, all the more as there are good reasons to doubt that John the *apostle* is the John who composed Revelation, but if John the Seer *did* have an assistant named Prochorus on Patmos, he could not have been the same Prochorus as the man selected by the apostles to help look after the widows in the Jerusalem almost sixty years before.

JOHN'S REMOVAL TO PATMOS

Though some have tried to argue that John was on Patmos "for the sake of [preaching] the word of God and the witness of Jesus" (Rev 1:2), it seems far more likely, and far more grammatically natural, to understand him to have been sent to Patmos "on account of" (Greek *dia*) his *prior* activity testifying to the word of God and to Jesus. Patmos was not much of an evangelistic opportunity, but it was a good place to which to remove a vocal dissident.

Exile or physical removal was a common enough punishment in the Roman world. Augustus famously exiled deviant members of his own family, sending them to tiny islands in the Mediterranean. Pandateria, for example, whither he exiled his sexually promiscuous daughter, Julia, is less than two miles long from tip to tip and about half a mile at its widest point. Such exile, called deportation (*deportatio*), was a capital sentence that involved loss of citizenship and confiscation of all property save for a modest living allowance. It lay only in the purview of the emperor (though provincial governors could petition the emperor for this sentence) or the prefect of Rome.

Another form of exile was relegation (*relegatio*), either *from* a locale, which left one's options rather more broad, or *to* a locale, which circumscribed the space where the sentenced person could live unmolested. Frequently, the latter involved *relegatio ad insulam*, being sentenced to live out one's days on a particular island. It did not involve loss of status or confiscation of property. This was a sentence that could be delivered by provincial governors and prefects, and it was frequently inveighed against philosophers, diviners, and other such troublemakers. John certainly fits into these categories, and it seems more likely that the emperor would not have become personally involved in the case of a local dissident in Ephesus.

> The size and congeniality of the island was often a measure of the leniency or severity of the sentence. Patmos was not a barren, uninhabited island. It was home to a sufficient population to support a gymnasium, a significant temple to Artemis, and likely a temple to Apollo. Excavations and explorations of the island have yielded no evidence of mines, quarries, or prisons. On the other hand, it is quite small (34 square kilometers). The proconsul did not show particular severity toward John, nor did he do John any favors by choosing Patmos for his exile, though it is remarkable that John was exiled rather than dispatched. The virulent anti-Roman prophet of the eastern Christ cult now found himself, for an indefinite period, on an island the circumference of which he could walk in twelve hours with perhaps a thousand residents to hear (and mostly reject) his ravings. One can only imagine the extent to which his pastoral heart was troubled for the congregations in whose lives he could no longer directly intervene.

"If you will gather your assembly," Prochorus said, "I'll read John's message to all of you—tonight, if at all possible. I need to take his word to my home congregation in Smyrna and on through the assemblies of Asia."

Amyntas gauged the earnestness in the faces of these men and nodded his acquiescence.

"Diodotos, help me spread the word to the rest of our assembly, and invite all who can to join us after sundown."

"In the meanwhile," said Prochorus, "if I might trouble you for ink and some parchment or papyrus, as I have a few hours I will make a copy of John's message to leave with you to share with the other congregations here after I move on to Smyrna."

"Of course, Prochorus. You may use the desk in my *tablinum*," Amyntas said, leading him to the room opposite the entrance.

"There are styluses and ink on top. I keep my supply of papyrus here in this box." Amyntas retrieved a few sheets from the box and laid them out on the desk. "If you need more, Menes here can fetch some from the market."

"Thank you, Amyntas."

Prochorus sat down immediately at the desk and began to unroll the parchment he had been carrying. Amyntas looked over his shoulder at the opening lines.

A revelation from Jesus Christ, which God gave him to show his slaves what must come to pass quickly . . .

6

The Day of Decision

6 Kaisaros, 4 Kalends October

The View from Above

Amyntas had not slept much that night. The little sleep he found had become a stage on which images from John's visions came alive again to play with other figures from Amyntas's memory and imagination.

He saw himself standing before the great cult statue in the Temple of Domitian, wearing a long white robe and the crown of an imperial priest. A crowd of worshipers stood about him, falling down before the image and chanting out, "Who is like you, our lord and god?" He saw Diodotos entering the temple and standing in front of him, shouting at him and at all the other worshipers, pointing to the heavens, but he could hear nothing of what he was saying. Then the cult image came to life, stepped down from its podium, and handed Amyntas its enormous spear, which became a spear of normal length in Amyntas's hand. He thrust the spear through Diodotos, who fell to the ground and dissolved into a pool of blood, and all the worshipers of the image stood up and cheered. He knelt, scooped up a small amount of the blood in a shallow bowl, and then poured it out over the fire on the altar before the image.

Then a great bowl appeared in the sky over their heads. As it was tipped, something like ash floated down on him and all the worshipers with him. It began to burn their flesh like hot cinders, down their very bones. As he fell, he saw Diodotos take shape again from the crimson pool, rise up from the floor, and lift his arms, praising the God of heaven. His voice drowned out all the anguished cries of the worshipers of the image.

Amyntas woke with a start, his nightclothes wet with perspiration, and determined that he would have no more dreams that night. He left his bedchamber as quietly as possible, so as not to disturb Chrysanthe, and walked along the hallway that overlooked their courtyard below toward the front of the house, where a previous owner had created access to the roof and a pleasant terrace surrounded by a balustrade. The air, not yet warmed by the first rays of the sun, chilled him as it blew against his damp clothes, awakening him fully.

He looked up the Embolos to the southeast, in the direction of the Temple of Domitian. Only the uppermost part of its tall roof was visible to him on account of the intervening residences, placed higher on the hill than his own. Nevertheless, he imagined it in its entirety as he had seen it a few days before, and he visualized the civic forum stretching out below it farther to the east with its Temple of Augustus and its shrine of Artemis and Julius. He held it all in his mind as he looked up into the vast, starry sky above those spaces, imagining the throne of God above and the myriad angels worshiping around it as described by John. How small the city's temples seemed, how marginal—how subversive, and yet how petty at the same time. And all those who gathered in those spaces were ignorant of the true center of the cosmos.

Nicolaus had been wrong. An idol indeed might be nothing, but getting thousands upon thousands of human beings, created in the image of the one God, to gather around and worship idols

DOMITIAN'S DIMINISHED POPULARITY AND EPHESUS'S FLAVIAN TEMPLE

The worship of Domitian in Ephesus, as elsewhere, was destined to be short-lived. Immediately following his assassination in AD 96, the army, whom Domitian had greatly favored, clamored for Domitian to be officially declared divine by the Senate. While living emperors could be worshiped as gods in the provinces, this was not done in Italy until after their deaths, and that only if the Senate had recognized them as *divi*, "deified," as it had previously done in the cases of Julius, Augustus, Claudius, Vespasian, and Titus.

The Senate, however, expressed unreserved relief and joy at Domitian's untimely demise and ordered the gold and silver statues of Domitian (signs of divinity) melted and repurposed, his commemorative triumphal arches pulled down, and his name stricken from public inscriptions to the extent possible. Such condemnation of a past (and particularly hated) ruler's memory, known in Latin as *damnatio me-*

Figure 6.1. An inscription from Gerasa (modern Jerash), a Decapolis city, showing Domitian's name to have been excised.

---

moriae, has ancient roots—for example, the nearly successful abolition of the names of Akhnaton and his line from the monuments of Egypt. Inscriptions across the Mediterranean testify to the punctiliousness with which the Senate's ruling was carried out.

Why Domitian met with such a fate is not entirely clear. Explanations tend to turn toward his general lack of civility, his un-Roman desire to be addressed as "lord" (*dominus*) and perhaps also as "god" (*deus*) in person and in correspondence, and an upturn in paranoia and severity toward the end of his reign (seen, for example, in his execution of several members of the senatorial class, including his own cousin, for their attraction to Judaism).

The temple in Ephesus seems to have been dedicated to multiple members of the Flavian family at once, as it is referred to as the "temple of the emperors" (the Sebastoi, or "Augustuses"). This likely included Vespasian and Titus, who immediately following AD 96 no longer had to share their cult with the disgraced Domitian in Ephesus's grand temple.

---

created in their own image and by their own hands—that was the work of the ancient enemy of the one God. He recalled something that Paul had written: *What they sacrifice, they sacrifice to demons and not to God.*

Amyntas walked over to the north balustrade, from which he had an enviable view of the lower city. He looked out along the Cardo leading to the north and over the commercial forum with its smaller, adjacent markets, and then beyond to the great road leading west to the harbor. He could see signs of activity already as the sky was just beginning to lighten, heralding the sun's resurgence on the horizon, still perhaps an hour away. Merchants, sailors, tradesmen of all kinds were already scrambling about, preparing more tribute to glut the desires of the great prostitute to the West. Now that he had heard John's vision—Prochorus had read it to the assembly the previous night—he would never look at a statue or frieze of the goddess Roma the same way—there was no "unseeing" the image of that insatiable, luxuriating whore. How much *had* Rome brought prosperity to Asia? How much more did Rome bleed Asia for its resources to satisfy its own desires? He had asked himself such questions before, but had never quite imagined the scale of the answer.

Blood. Amyntas thought about the martyrs under the altar in heaven calling out for vindication. He thought about the blood in the prostitute's cup, the blood that inebriated her, that she craved as if addicted. He had heard so much about peace since he was a child. No number of reports about war and revolt had ever really moved him to question the "peace" that Rome brought. But now he thought about the stories John had told about the doomed revolt in Judea, the scenes of carnage after desperately one-sided battles, the slow starvation of tens of thousands of innocents trapped in Jerusalem during the final siege. He thought about the stories from Ephesus's own past, how at the instigation of King Mithridates of Pontus they had revolted themselves against Roman rule and paid dearly for it over a century and a half ago. And now, here they all were, honoring Rome as a protective goddess and her rulers as beneficent gods, praising them as the bringers of nothing save peace, order, wealth, and rule of law, ignoring the bodies piled upon bodies that were the mortar between the bricks of empire. He thought of the wrath that burned against Rome for all her crimes, and looked to the sky, half expecting to see the plagues of a great new exodus beginning to fall from heaven.

His reflections were interrupted by the sound of sandals on the plastered wood behind him. He turned to see Chrysanthe approaching, wrapped in a woolen blanket. She walked to the balustrade next to her husband and leaned against him affectionately.

"Not sleeping?" she asked.

"Not well. Troubling dreams."

"I have been dreaming as well. And thinking." Chrysanthe paused. "I couldn't get John's words—*Jesus'* words—out of my head: 'You have abandoned your first love.'"

"Those stuck with me as well," Amyntas said. "And the consequences for our assemblies—'Remember whence you have fallen and repent, lest I come and remove your lampstand from its place,' or something like that."

"There wasn't a great deal of love in our assembly two nights ago."

"No, indeed," Amyntas concurred. "Some of our brothers are clear enough as to where the lines are drawn, and *right* enough about those lines, it would appear, but seem to have lost the ability to love *across* those lines."

They stood together in silence for a few moments. Amyntas pondered other meanings that Jesus' warning might carry for him. *Do I love* God *enough to keep even his first and most basic commandment? Do I love the men in the assembly enough to tell them the truth about what they're doing, to* warn *them about the dangers they do not see?*

The first rays of the sun were slicing through the darkness in the sky above them. Amyntas looked down at the waist-high wall on which he'd been resting his hands and rubbed his finger over a bit of graffiti cut by a previous resident into the plaster.

Rome, queen over all, your power will never end.[1]

"I've seen that a hundred times," said Chrysanthe. "I keep meaning to ask Menes to plaster over it."

---

[1] This graffito (*IEph* 599, cited in J. Nelson Kraybill, *Apocalypse and Allegiance: Worship, Politics, and Devotion in the Book of Revelation* [Grand Rapids: Brazos, 2010], 57) was actually found in the interior of one of the terrace houses, the upper floors and roof gardens of which have not survived.

"I have as well. I've always read it as a something the scribbler was happily affirming. I wonder now if it might have been a remark of despair."

"Come downstairs, husband," she said gently, putting her hand on his arm. "I'll make you breakfast, and then we can spend some time in prayer together."

"I'll be right down," he replied, as Chrysanthe descended the stairs into the house. He looked up along the Embolos again and thought about the city council that would meet later that day and the courage it would take to stand before them.

But, looking up to the sky, he thought of the day when God would tear open the heavens, when all would stand before him and his Anointed—before whom no one would be able to stand confidently who had not first stood courageously for him here below.

IN THE COUNCIL CHAMBER

An hour before the sun had reached its zenith, Amyntas walked up the Embolos and stood at the far west end of the Basilica Stoa across from the Prytaneion, lingering there as was his custom.

"In you, O Lord, I have put my trust," he said quietly. "Let me not be put to shame."

After a few minutes, the acolyte reemerged from the council chamber and returned to the Prytaneion with the sacred flame, signaling that the council's opening rites had ended.

Amyntas gathered his resolve and entered the chamber, quietly making his way to a seat in one of the upper tiers as Claudianus launched into the business of the day.

"Aristion has brought a proposal for the council's consideration —and I think it's a good one: that we broaden the requirement of an annual oath of loyalty to our emperor. Aristion, would you care to say more?"

"Thank you, noble Claudianus," Aristion said as he rose to address the council. "Up to now it has only been our practice to require an annual oath of loyalty to be taken by members of each guild associated with a particular trade or business, as these assemblies have often proved to be the seedbed of sedition. I am proposing that we extend the requirement to *every* regular assembly in our city, whether our own body here, the youth enrolled in the gymnasium, colleges of priests, any group meeting regularly for religious purposes, whatever the purpose."

"Aristion has proposed a slightly adapted text for this oath," Claudianus said. "Would you read it for us?"

"Certainly. 'I swear by Jupiter and all the gods and goddesses, and by the emperor himself, that I will be loyal to the divine emperor Domitian and his house in thought, word, and deed as long as I live. I will regard the emperor's friends as my own; his enemies I will regard as my enemies. I will withhold neither goods nor life nor children in the defense of his interests.' We can allow the Jews to adapt the language and swear by their own God, of course."

"You mean the Jews who are *truly* Jews?"

"Yes, indeed, Serapion," Aristion said. "Those who are duly enrolled and who pay the *fiscus Iudaicus* imposed on their kind by the divine Vespasian after their insurrection."

"As Ephesus is now the *neōkoros* of the province-wide cult of the divine Domitian," Claudianus said, "it is fitting that every group within the city walls pledge themselves to him."

"And what of assemblies that do *not* swear such an oath?" inquired Serapion.

"Ephesus will *have* no such assemblies . . . assembling," answered Claudianus. "Do we need further discussion, or are we prepared to vote?"

Affirmative murmurs and gestures throughout the room gave Claudianus his answer.

THE *FISCUS IUDAICUS* AND THE "SYNAGOGUE OF SATAN"

While it stood, the temple in Jerusalem was subsidized, at least in part, by an annual levy of two drachmas (two denarii) paid by faithful Jewish males between the ages of twenty and fifty across the empire. An episode in Matthew 17:24-27 speaks of these "dues" (often referred to as the "temple tax") and the expectation that good Jews would participate willingly.

After the suppression of the Jewish Revolt of AD 66–70, the emperor Vespasian imposed war reparations on the Jewish people in a peculiar fashion. He decreed that Jews would continue to pay the *didrachmon*, formerly paid for the maintenance and operations of their temple, to the imperial treasury. In the first instance, these funds would now be designated for the final stages of the rebuilding and the ongoing maintenance of the great temple of Jupiter Capitolinus, the heart of the Roman state religion, towering symbolically above the Roman Forum. Vespasian dramatically increased the range of persons liable to the tax (now officially called the *fiscus Iudaicus*, the "Jewish tax")—henceforth Jews of *both* genders from the age of four through at least the age of sixty. The total

Figure 6.2. A silver cistophorus of Titus celebrating the completion of the renovations of the Temple of Capitoline Jupiter. Courtesy of the Classical Numismatic Group, LLC.

amount was upwards of ten million denarii and was no doubt used to fund a wide range of projects, but its connection with the Temple of Jupiter, Juno, and Minerva on the Capitoline Hill was firmly fixed, such that both the historians Josephus (*Jewish War* 7.218) and Dio Cassius (*Roman History* 46.7.2) mention this explicitly.[a]

We can only speculate how Jews felt about the penalty. From one perspective, the penalty could be seen as an expression of leniency toward a rebellious nation, though Vespasian could not have been ignorant of the religious signification of thus shifting the *didrachmon*'s beneficiary. It seems reasonable, however, to suppose that some Jews would have found it an intolerable imposition to be expected quite literally to render unto Caesar what had been due unto God. An uncompromising Jew such as John the Seer might well have regarded this as an outright betrayal on the part of his fellow Jews, who ought to have refused to purchase forgiveness and toleration through their subvention of an idolatrous cult—indeed, the cult of the chief Roman antigod, Jupiter or, in John's worldview, Satan. When John speaks of the local Jewish community as a "synagogue of Satan" (Rev 2:9; 3:9), this might strike modern readers as unduly vitriolic. We should remember, however, that such accusations are not unprecedented among rival Jewish movements. The Qumran sectarians referred to Jews outside their group as "the congregation of Beliar" (Dead Sea Scrolls 1QH 2.22; 1QM 4.9), one of Satan's *noms de guerre*, and Jesus is remembered to have called his (fellow Jewish) opponents "children of Satan" (Jn 8:44).

---

[a]See further Mary Smallwood, *The Jews Under Roman Rule from Pompey to Diocletian* (Leiden, Netherlands: Brill, 1981), 371-76.

"All in favor, then, of Aristion's proposal?"

"Aye," thundered the room.

"Opposed?"

Amyntas knew there was no point in speaking.

"Aristion's proposal passes," declared Claudianus. "We can discuss implementation at a future meeting, though I would suggest we consider requiring the oath every year in the month of Apellaios, the month of Domitian's birthday, as the most suitable time."

"Indeed, it should be Apellaios," Montanus chimed in, "and it should begin *this* Apellaios. What better complement to the inauguration of the Temple of Domitian than for all the city's assemblies to affirm their loyalty to our divine emperor?"

"Perhaps this is indeed an easy matter," said Claudianus. "Is there anyone present who sees reason to defer implementation or to suggest a different date?"

Once again, the room signaled its contentment to move ahead and be done with the matter.

"All right, then. We will receive this as a sign of consensus," concluded Claudianus. "And as we're already thinking about the subject of our new temple, Amyntas—"

Amyntas's pulse quickened.

"—do you have an answer for us? Will you accept the honor of joining the college of *neōpoioi* for Domitian's temple, a modest honor, perhaps, but no doubt only the first in a long and distinguished series to come?"

Amyntas hesitantly half stood to give his answer.

"Regretfully, I cannot."

As soon as the words left his lips, he sat down again.

"What's this, then, Amyntas?" Serapion said above the low murmur that had begun to erupt around the room. "Surely the duties are not *so* burdensome that you *cannot* take them on. We would have some explanation from you!"

A number of other voices affirmed the demand.

Amyntas closed his eyes, drew in a deep breath, and rose to his full height as he exhaled. He opened his eyes and looked into the faces around the chamber.

"I can remember how, some eleven years ago, a week of public mourning was declared for the 'divine' Vespasian. And then, just two years later, another week of mourning was declared for the 'divine' Titus. Even if Domitian should reign as long as Augustus did, such a week of mourning will one day also be decreed for him."

He paused for a moment and looked down, rubbing his fingertips together, as if trying to recollect something.

"Xenophanes of Colophon said it best: 'If they are gods, do not mourn them; if they are mortals, do not sacrifice to them.'"

"Xenophanes was talking about the barbaric superstitions of the Egyptians, Amyntas," objected Serapion.

"And he would object as forcefully to the superstitions we are inventing here with our worship of human beings like ourselves. The emperor may be the ruler of land and sea, but he's also just a man. An eight-meter-high colossus doesn't change that. A temple with a priesthood doesn't change that. What drives us to want to play out such a charade?"

Serapion caught and held Amyntas's eye. There was no mistaking the smug, self-gratulation in his look.

"I am dismayed to hear such words coming from your mouth, Amyntas," said Claudianus. "If you harbored such impiety in your heart, you could at least have told us at once and not raised our hopes."

"Impiety, noble Claudianus?" Amyntas objected. "Domitian did not give us life. Domitian did not set the good array of creation in order to provide for our every need. But there *is* a God in heaven who did these things, and which of you gives him the worship and pious obedience that is *his* due?"

"Amyntas speaks of the tribal god of the Jews, I think," Serapion commented.

"I speak of the one true, living God who made heaven, earth, and all that is therein," Amyntas declared. "I speak of the God who will hold all his creatures accountable when he comes to judge the earth and its inhabitants. And I urge you all to consider the invitation he has given to us all, to be reconciled to him in the name of his Son, Jesus the Christ."

The hostile grumbling throughout the chamber conspired to drown out Amyntas's final words. Finally Claudianus was able to bring the room back to a semblance of order.

"Even the Epicureans can *pretend* to be pious for the sake of solidarity with their fellow citizens. But you cannot even do that in honor of our sensibilities."

Aristion rose to speak.

"Noble Claudianus, a man who does not honor our gods does not deserve a voice in this chamber."

A surge of assent arose across the assembly.

"There is no such stipulation in our constitution, noble Aristion. Nevertheless," Claudianus said with a hint of menace, "it would be a foolish man to remain where he is so unwelcome."

A heavy silence followed. Amyntas's posture slowly relaxed in a reflex of resignation. The eyes of everyone in the assembly were on him as he rose to his feet and began to make his way to the nearest stairway and down through the assembly. He could hear the derogatory remarks of those closest to him above the general jeering of the body. As he walked out of the council chamber, he heard Serapion's voice rising above the rest.

"We have been tolerant far too long. The disappearance of piety toward the gods will eventually mean the disappearance of loyalty and unity among people and the decay of all justice. We need to cleanse our city of such pollution . . ."

7

The Day After

7 Kaisaros, 3 Kalends October

Business as Usual

It was the third hour of the day before Demetrius entered the commercial forum. His heart had not been in his business since he had heard the message Prochorus bore from John the Seer, and it manifested in procrastination. He knew his workers would get the shop opened up and set out any new merchandise received from his suppliers inland. He could not shake the image that had sunk its roots into his mind—that the supply and distribution chains of the empire, of which he was one small node, were just so many endless lines of ants in a giant hive channeling all the resources of the world toward the great, parasitic queen at its center.

As he made his way through the great South Gate and walked along the south portico of the forum, he saw nothing but hundreds of bipedal ants carrying the leaves and larvae for their distant queen. He passed Diodotos, at work in his shop, carefully cutting stone and tiles into pieces for a new mosaic he had been commissioned to create. They always involved geometric designs, perhaps the occasional images of fish or birds, but never any motifs from the stories of the false gods and their exploits.

Diodotos had his own boundaries, and he never transgressed them. Demetrius felt a brief pang of envy.

He came at last to his own shop and, for the first time, felt embarrassment rather than pride that his business had expanded to occupy four storefronts. *Quite the successful worker ant.*

"Good morning, Demetrius," said Kleon, his shop manager.

"Good morning, Kleon."

"More wares arrived this morning from Laodicea and Hierapolis, and just in time, too. That Italian negotiator came by yesterday afternoon after you left, having just returned from Miletus. I haven't unpacked anything, as I wanted to know from you first how much of this would be going with him."

Demetrius thought for a moment and scanned the crowd in the forum. His eyes lighted on their target, and he took several strides out into the open square.

"Timon!" he called out, cupping his hands around his mouth.

He took a few more steps and shouted out again. Timon heard his name and turned toward Demetrius, who waved him over to his shop. Timon held up his index finger to signal that he'd come as soon as he had finished the transaction in which he was engaged.

"Kleon, open those two bags, and let's spread some of the goods on the table here."

As Demetrius and Kleon were arranging a number of woolen garments on the display table, Timon stepped up into the portico.

"Ah, Timon," Demetrius said, "we've just received a shipment from inland. Is there still demand in Colophon for garments."

"Of course, Demetrius. I've not been able to acquire anything since last week."

"How many can you use?"

"Two dozen or so, easily—but what about your Italian buyer?"

"It would be least awkward if we could finish up our business before he arrives."

"I can't match his price of eight denarii per garment."

"The usual five denarii will be sufficient, Timon."

Timon was having visible difficulty processing all of this.

"Rome doesn't need all the wool in Asia," Demetrius said. "The people of Colophon deserve some, and you need to make your living as well."

Timon smiled, counted out 120 denarii, and walked away happily with twenty-four garments piled high in his arms.

"Congratulations, Demetrius. You managed to throw away seventy-two denarii before midday!"

Demetrius turned to see Flavius Zeuxis leaning against a column of the portico.

"Good morning, Zeuxis. I was feeling bad that Timon got shut out last week. There's still plenty here to sell to the Italian for his buyers, and at the price he's paying I can afford to deal fairly with some of our locals."

"I understand, Demetrius. One must often weigh the profit of silver against the profit of maintaining a relationship. Meanwhile the goats of the Lycus Valley are busy turning more grass into wool for us."

Demetrius considered Zeuxis for a moment.

"How do you, as a Jew, come to terms with serving the interests of Rome as you do, when she has shed so much Jewish blood?"

"Philanthropist and philosopher, all on the same morning!" Zeuxis laughed and then paused thoughtfully. "Well, Demetrius, mine is not the first generation of Jews that had to learn how to survive scattered throughout a Gentile world. The instruction that Jeremiah gave to our people over six centuries ago still seems good advice to me—'Build houses and live in them; plant gardens and eat their produce. Take wives and have children; multiply there, and do not dwindle.'"

Zeuxis became somewhat more serious as he continued.

"I don't deal in incense or sell other such supplies to Gentiles as might be used in their idol worship.[1] I refuse to transport slaves or otherwise profit from the sale of lives—they are not mere 'bodies,' as dealers and buyers like to say. I have used Rome's insatiable hunger to feed my family and provide stability for the many who have become in some way dependent on me."

Demetrius nodded to signal his acceptance of his friend's explanation. Zeuxis leaned in closer to him.

"The day may indeed come when God remembers Rome's crimes against her, but, until then," he added with a good-natured laugh, "she remains a great dog on which the fleas can suck and fatten themselves, does she not? We fleas must look out for one another and use the dog to our best advantage in the interim, no?"

"Indeed, Zeuxis, indeed," Demetrius conceded. "I have become concerned of late that we not facilitate injustice in our catering to this great and quite ravenous dog. Have you considered, for example, what your plans for the cinnamon trade will do to the people in Taprobane?"

"Besides make their cinnamon dealers rich?"

"Yes, like putting cinnamon out of the reach of the people there where it's grown."

"Demetrius, it literally grows on trees there. And even if they were to export it *all* to Rome for the profit, well, I've never heard of anyone dying from a lack of cinnamon—and it might make it easier for them to buy what *does* sustain life."

Zeuxis leaned in a bit closer and lowered his voice.

"And the profits from our trade will help you look after those people who gather in your house." Zeuxis clapped his younger friend on the shoulder. "The *Leviathan* is riding at winter

---

[1]See 'Abodah Zar. 1.13b, 14b. Tertullian also so advised Christian merchants (*Idol.* 11; see J. Nelson Kraybill, *Imperial Cult and Commerce in John's Apocalypse* [Sheffield: Sheffield Academic, 1996], 191).

anchorage, and I'm anxious to return to my own home in Hierapolis, sleep next to my own wife, and see my landlubberly sons. Come visit us there, Demetrius. We'll talk more."

The two men embraced each other, and Zeuxis was off.

Demetrius began to put the few garments Timon had not purchased back into the large canvas bags in which they had been delivered to await the Italian's arrival. As he did so, he moved back and forth in his mind between Zeuxis's vision for their business together and the vision he had heard read to him two nights before. Would it be possible to *flirt* with the great prostitute and not be sucked in and polluted? If he gained access to significantly greater wealth, he might indeed be in a position to sustain fellow Christians when their faith brought them into difficulty. But would the wealth and everything, everyone it touched be tainted? Demetrius knew one thing for certain: he would have to learn more about cinnamon and what its trade did for—or did *to*—the people in far-off Taprobane before he could make up his mind.

He was recalled from his musings as Hermotimus the *agoranomos*, accompanied by four members of his "security team," as he called his thugs, pushed through the South Stoa, heading for Diodotos's stall.

"Be it known to all men of honor and virtue present," Hermotimus shouted, "that complaints have been lodged against Diodotos for breaches of agreements and for delaying delivery of product to negotiate higher fees. As I am entrusted with protecting those who frequent this market, I can't allow such a person to remain in business in this space. Diodotos, your lease is hereby canceled. Anything still on the premises on the tenth of the month will be confiscated."

"Who is accusing me?" shouted a stunned Diodotos. "Where is your evidence?"

"You have every right to face your accusers and file a pro-
ceeding in the courts," Hermotimus conceded, "though neither
the gods nor Justice herself could possibly smile on an atheist
such as yourself."

Diodotos immediately understood the implication.

"Moreover," the *agoranomos* continued, "Diodotos is hereby
expelled from the guild of mosaic makers and interior artists."

Diodotos was about to voice another objection when Hermotimus silenced him with a gesture.

"Don't act surprised, Diodotos. It's long overdue, given your
conspicuous absence from most guild functions—or your conspicuously *tardy* appearance after their rites of pious devotion
to the gods and the emperor are ended."

Hermotimus leaned closer to the artisan.

"Better just to move on," he advised, "and get a fresh start
elsewhere."

He signaled to one of his thugs who, equipped with mallet and
chisel, walked across the forum toward the west portico, on
whose walls were engraved the membership rosters of the city's
various trade guilds.

Hermotimus and his remaining posse returned to his second-
story office. Demetrius watched Diodotos for a few moments
and then walked over to his stall.

"'In order that no one might buy or sell who does not have the
mark of the monster'—or something like that."

Diodotos nodded, remembering the warning from John's
message.

"If I can be of any help to you, please come see me," Demetrius
offered. "I have good connections in Hierapolis and its neighboring cities."

Still stunned, Diodotos could only nod again.

Demetrius turned and took a few steps in the direction of his
own shop when Diodotos's voice halted him.

"'If anyone worships the monster and its image and receives its mark, that person will also drink from wine of God's wrath and be tormented with fire and sulfur before the holy angels and before the Lamb.'"

Demetrius turned again to look at Diodotos.

"Indeed, Diodotos. And we must pray that not even Hermotimus comes to such an end, if our light here is to remain."

A GRACE DEFACED

Amyntas sat at the desk in the *tablinum*, staring at the stack of papyrus leaves on which Prochoros had copied John's message. He had not set foot outside his house since the previous afternoon and had no intentions of venturing out today. Keeping Secundus home from his lessons at the gymnasium had been an obvious decision. He was considering closing up the townhouse and taking his family to spend a few weeks at their farm estate.

The sound of a hand slapping against the outer door summoned Amyntas to the present. He rose and crossed the atrium.

"Who is it?"

"It's me, *dominus*. Menes."

"Are you alone?"

"Yes, *dominus*."

Amyntas opened the door.

"Are you back from the market so soon?"

"No, *dominus*. I . . . I think there's something you should see."

Amyntas heaved a sigh at the prospect of having to go out after all. "Chrysanthe?" he called.

His wife appeared in a window of a second-floor room overlooking the atrium.

"Please come down and bolt the door behind me. I need to go with Menes."

Chrysanthe nodded.

"God watch over you both," she said, as she disappeared from the window and made for the stairway beside the courtyard.

Menes pulled the door shut behind them so that it latched and led Amyntas down the narrow stairway that gave access to the townhouses to the Embolos. The two followed the Cardo toward the theater.

Most of the pedestrian traffic ignored them, which was a relief to Amyntas. He only saw a reflection of his disgrace in the face of an occasional passer-by.

As Menes led him in the direction of the fountain Amyntas had been restoring, Amyntas began to suspect what had happened, and when the fountain came into view, his forebodings were confirmed. During the night, someone had taken to its façade with a heavy mallet. Pieces of the decorative work along the low-rise architrave—the costliest part of the renovation— were scattered on the pavement in front of the fountain. He

Figure 7.1. The Hellenistic-period fountain located at the head of Harbor Street.

scanned the dedicatory inscription running across the architrave. The portion bearing Amyntas's name had been demolished. Above the space where his name had been, someone had painstakingly scratched "A hater of the gods."

He peered into the fountain house itself and saw the single word, painted with a bright red pigment: "Ungrateful." Amyntas understood that this was meant as an accusation against him, but it struck him also as a self-incrimination of the vandals themselves, this utter rejection of his desire to beautify his city.

No, he silently corrected himself, *not my city anymore.*

Amyntas turned away from the fountain and looked down Harbor Street at the hundreds of people making their way up and down, many dragging some cargo or other. He looked to the end of the street to the harbor itself, and beyond it, toward Rome. He imagined once again the vast scene of the worship of the one God and the Lamb by the myriad angels of heaven in the skies above the west. He felt a surge both of panic at what further consequences might follow yesterday's decision and, for perhaps the first time, an intense longing for the realm whose citizen he had now declared himself. From deep within arose a prayer that escaped his lips before he was even aware.

"Come, Lord Jesus."

FOR FURTHER STUDY

deSilva, David. *AR271: The Seven Cities of Revelation*. Logos Mobile Education. Bellingham, WA: Lexham, 2018.

———. *Seeing Things John's Way: The Rhetoric of the Book of Revelation*. Louisville, KY: Westminster John Knox, 2009.

———. *Unholy Allegiances: Heeding Revelation's Warning*. Peabody, MA: Hendrickson, 2013.

Fairchild, Mark. *Christian Origins in Ephesus and Asia Minor*. Peabody, MA: Hendrickson, 2017.

Friesen, Steven. *Imperial Cults and the Apocalypse of John: Reading Revelation in the Ruins*. Oxford: Oxford University Press, 2001.

———. *Twice Neokoros: Ephesus, Asia and the Cult of the Flavian Imperial Family*. Leiden, Netherlands: Brill, 1993.

Koester, Craig. *Revelation: A New Translation with Introduction and Commentary*. Anchor Yale Bible 38A. New Haven, CT: Yale University Press, 2014.

Koester, Helmut, ed. *Ephesos: Metropolis of Asia*. Harvard Theological Studies 41. Valley Forge, PA: Trinity Press International, 1995.

Kraybill, J. Nelson. *Apocalypse and Allegiance: Worship, Politics, and Devotion in the Book of Revelation*. Grand Rapids: Brazos, 2010.

———. *Imperial Cult and Commerce in John's Apocalypse*. Sheffield, England: Sheffield Academic, 1996.

Murphy O'Connor, Jerome. *St. Paul's Ephesus: Texts and Archaeology*. Collegeville, MN: Michael Glazier, 2008.

Price, S. R. F. *Rituals and Power: The Roman Imperial Cult in Asia Minor*. Cambridge: Cambridge University Press, 1984.

Scherrer, Peter. *Ephesus: The New Guide*. Istanbul: Ege Yayınları, 2000.

Trebilco, Paul. *The Early Christians in Ephesus from Paul to Ignatius*. Grand Rapids: Eerdmans, 2007.

OTHER BOOKS BY
DAVID deSILVA

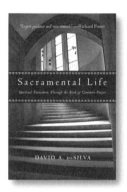 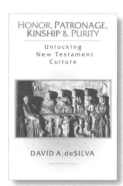 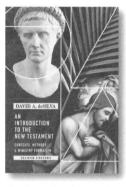

Sacramental Life
978-0-8308-3518-8

Honor, Patronage,
Kinship & Purity
978-0-8308-1572-2

An Introduction to the
New Testament
978-0-8308-5217-8

Other Books in the Series

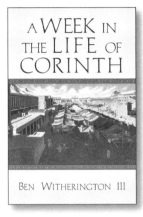

A WEEK IN THE LIFE OF CORINTH

BEN WITHERINGTON III

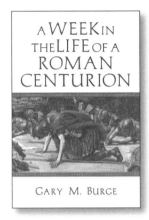

A WEEK IN THE LIFE OF A ROMAN CENTURION

GARY M. BURGE

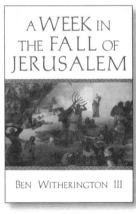

A WEEK IN THE FALL OF JERUSALEM

BEN WITHERINGTON III

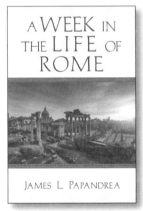

A WEEK IN THE LIFE OF ROME

JAMES L. PAPANDREA

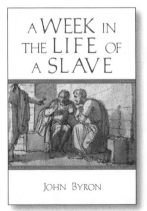

A WEEK IN THE LIFE OF A SLAVE

JOHN BYRON

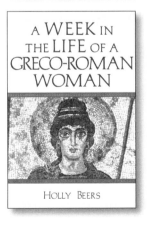

A WEEK IN THE LIFE OF A GRECO-ROMAN WOMAN

HOLLY BEERS

Finding the Textbook You Need

The IVP Academic Textbook Selector
is an online tool for instantly finding the IVP books
suitable for over 250 courses across 24 disciplines.

---

ivpacademic.com
